True Gold

True Gold

Cliff Rennie

CF4·K

© Copyright 1992 Cliff Rennie
ISBN 978-1-84550-655-1

Published in 1992,
reprinted in 2004 and 2011
by
Christian Focus Publications
Geanies House, Fearn,
Ross-shire, IV20 1TW,
Great Britain

www.christianfocus.com
email: info@christianfocus.com

Cover design by Alister MacInnes
Cover illustration and other illustrations by
Jonathan Williams
Printed and bound by Nørhaven, Denmark

To
Lieutenant Commander Rupert Craven
of Bettyhill, whose hospitality has been
enjoyed by many.

Acknowledgements
To
Bill and Nessie Rose.

Contents

Bettyhill Beach

'Come on into the water, Mum, it's lovely and cool.' Gillian Reynolds was obviously having the time of her life. So excited was she that Sue and Paul, her parents, found they just had to lay aside their towels and take the plunge into the Atlantic waters that girdle the north coast of the County of Sutherland.

Yes, this was Scotland. Sue Reynolds could hardly come to terms with it. The azure sky, the turquoise waters lapping on the white sands of a beach that still awaited discovery by the masses. Here was beauty, warmth and peace.

'Jason, you pig, stop it.' Gillian was being splashed by her brother who, being nearly two years older than her, assumed that he had a special right to be a nuisance to the younger ones. Unfortunately for Jason, his sister didn't share that belief and soon had her brother howling with discomfort as she flung handfuls of cold spray in his face.

The other members of the Reynolds family were running out of the water to meet their parents. Little Mike, aged eight-and-a-half, was holding one end of a blue and white rope he had found washed up on the shore from the previous night's tide. On the other end of the rope was Mega, the family's young Labrador. She was having the time of her life despite the attentions of Michelle, the daughter of friends of the family. Michelle was trying to slow Mega down by pulling her tail, a very unwise thing to do but for the placid nature of the friendly dog, whose wagging tail was proving too much for the little girl to hold.

'Mum, Mum,' cried little Mike with obvious pleasure. 'This is a fantastic place. Can we stay here for ever, or at least till school goes back?'

'Dad, is this what the Garden of Eden was like?' asked Gillian.

Before Paul could answer, he was faced with another request. Mega had shaken herself loose from Michelle's attentions and having laid down the shabby blue and white rope at *the boss*'s feet, was barking an enthusiastic invitation to a tug-of-war. It was Mum who came to the rescue, suggesting that they have a drink of lemonade and something to eat before exploring the shore and sand-dunes any further.

It was a fantastic place, as Mike had said. The children were in their element as they tore back and forth across the beach. They stopped occasionally to show their parents shells or stones they had found, or to ask them yet another question which had suddenly suggested itself on them. So the afternoon passed lazily on with the surge of waves and the cry of the seagulls circling overhead as they looked for welcome scraps.

At last it was time to go home, back over the dunes and up the little hill to the holiday cottage where they were staying. It was a small, well-built place that had two bedrooms for the children and a sitting room which doubled up as a bedroom for Paul and Sue at night. There was neither running water nor electricity.

Water had to be fetched from a nearby well, and there were oil lamps and a stove which was fuelled with an endless supply of peat stacked at the back door. Sue's heart had sunk when she first saw it, but she had quickly seen the advantages. The water was far better than anything she had ever drunk from a tap, and the children loved fetching it. The peat kindled easily, building up a good steady heat in the stove and enabling her to do all the cooking necessary on these lovely summer days.

Furthermore, the lamps were good enough for the simple reason that it hardly gets dark at all on the north coast in summer.

The children arrived home at teatime, starving. They wolfed down egg and chips, agreeing noisily between mouthfuls that 'nothing tastes as good as chips made by Mum.'

Tea was just over when a knock at the door announced the arrival of Mr Sinclair, the bailiff, whose job it was to look after the river and see that no one stole or 'poached' fish.

Mr Sinclair was a big man with a craggy, weather-beaten face. He had spent most of his life working out-of-doors 'helping fishermen and hunting poachers' as he put it. Mike noticed that the man had a jolly laugh and was fond of telling stories. After Mr Sinclair had gone the children helped to wash the dishes before going out to play. The long evening was lovely, with only the occasional sound of birds and insects to disturb the quietness, or the bleating of a lamb which had become separated from its mother as it played on the hillside.

'Oh, Mr Reynolds, this is a wonderful place' said Michelle. 'I must tell my Mum and Dad all about it. How I wish they could be here.'

'Why don't you send them a postcard, Michelle?' replied Paul. 'I bought a few at the Post Office this afternoon. Here you are, have this one. It shows the beach where you were playing and I was trying to relax!

You write a message on it and we'll all sign it after you.'

Michelle was so happy. She had known the Reynolds family for as long as she could remember and had always felt so much at home with them. She had no brothers or sisters and no dog, but with the Reynolds she had all three. She enjoyed going to church with her own parents and the Reynolds.

All good things must come to an end, even a long, warm fun-filled day in a place like Bettyhill.

Mum and Dad Reynolds finally managed to herd the last protesting member of their brood into the house for the night. There was a bath which the children filled for themselves and which proved very popular. It was one thing, however, to go to bed, it was another to fall asleep.

One member of the family who was having more trouble dropping off than the others was Jason. Against his parents' advice he had left his tee-shirt off just a little too long, and as a result was suffering from sunburn. Although his shoulders weren't too sore they certainly were itchy and uncomfortable. No matter how he tossed and turned, he couldn't quite get off to sleep.

Just as dawn was breaking at about 3 am, and when tiredness was taking over, Jason heard Mega begin to growl.

'Go back to sleep, Mega,' he mumbled.

'Woof,' replied the dog, rising from her rug at the end of his bed and moving to the window.

'Quiet, dog, or you'll wake the whole house,' protested Jason, looking across to the other bed to see if Mega had woken Mike. Mega continued to growl. Was there a prowler? Jason was frightened by the very thought and tried to shut it out of his mind. Nevertheless, he must check, just in case. Making a way past his sleeping brother, he parted the curtains over so slightly. What he saw made him tremble and gasp.

A group of about half a dozen shadowy figures were passing by on the moor, about a hundred yards from the house. They were carrying boxes between them, which seemed heavy. Who were they? What were they transporting? Where were they going? The questions scrambled untidily through Jason's tired, confused mind. Instinctively he wanted to wake the family, especially Dad, but a number of things made him hesitate.

In the first place, whoever these people were, they were moving away from the house. They didn't plan to break in or hurt Jason and his family. At the same time there was something sinister going on, and Jason didn't want to tangle with them if he could possibly avoid it.

Of even more importance to the frightened young boy at that moment was keeping the family dog quiet. Mega was sure that something was up. She knew that there were people out there and sensed the fear of her young master. Mega's canine sense of duty demanded that she bark the place down. However, that was not proving exactly easy as Jason's hand had closed round her muzzle and he was forbidding her to bark. Very unwillingly, but with remarkable obedience, the trembling dog settled down again on her rug.

After about ten minutes Jason turned back to the window and looked out again. Whoever had been out there on the moor had now disappeared. All was still and quiet, except Jason's beating heart and Mega's growls of frustration.

'There's only one thing to do about this,' said Jason to Mega. 'I'll tell Mum and Dad in the morning and they will know how to handle it.' They always did. Jason had never known what it was to have worries or fears or doubts that he could not share with his parents. They always understood and always had answers. Above all, they always cared.

How they would solve this problem the young lad didn't know, but he wasn't too worried because he knew that God would help them. Only that very night in their Bible reading from Isaiah chapter 41, Dad had read a verse that now came back to Jason. 'Fear not for I am with you.'

With that comforting thought, Jason wrapped the duvet around him, put his head on the pillow, and was soon off to sleep.

To The Rescue

Jason's parents didn't make too much of their son's story when he told them about the strange figures on the moor. Privately, however, Sue was concerned.

'Surely they could be up to no good at that time of night, and what do you think they were carrying?' she asked her husband.

'Don't know,' replied Paul thoughtfully. 'There's probably a reasonable explanation. Things may happen differently in a small country place where everyone knows everybody else. After all, it was light enough for them to be seen crossing the moor. We're not used to honest people moving about at three in the morning, but then we're not used to daylight at that time either.'

'I expect you're right,' said Sue only slightly more reassured, but her worries returned when they recounted Jason's experiences to Mr Sinclair. The bailiff had called in to see if they had slept well, but his friendly face quickly clouded over as he heard the story.

'Poachers,' he said firmly, 'must be.'

'But what would they be carrying in those boxes?' asked Paul. 'They sound more like pirates to me.'

Mr Sinclair chuckled. 'It's amazing how heavy the salmon can be, and those poaching rings net scores of them at a time. They are very selfish and really spoil things for the honest fishermen.'

'Then, you don't think there's anything dangerous or sinister about them?' asked Sue, a look of relief beginning to return to her features.

'Oh no, I hardly think so,' said the bailiff. 'I'll speak to the sergeant about it when I see him later today. It may be that they were disturbed and decided to hide their catch in the caves for a few hours. I doubt if we'll find any evidence; they usually cover their tracks very well. We'll have a look anyway.'

'You mean there are caves on the other side of the moor?' interrupted Paul.

'Och, they're nothing elaborate. They date back to the days of the Clearances, nearly two hundred years ago. It was the time when the crofters were turned out of their homes and had to move down to the shore. Until they built other houses some of them stayed for a short time in these caves.'

'How terrible!' exclaimed Sue. 'Why were they put out of their homes? What had they done?'

'They hadn't done anything wrong, Mrs Reynolds,' replied the bailiff. 'The landowners just felt they could make better use of the ground by giving it over to the sheep.'

'So the families were thrown out?' echoed Paul. 'Didn't they do anything about it?'

'Oh, they tried, but there was very little they could do, since the landowners had the government on their side. They were brave men. In the glen you can see a monument that tells how an army regiment was raised around that time. Years later the regiment gained six Victoria Crosses at the Battle of Lucknow in India. No English or Scottish regiment ever did better. They were brave people, but they were evicted for all that.'

At that point the children came in looking for food, hungry as usual. Mr Sinclair took his leave, and Mum was soon heating waffles and buttering bread while Dad poured drinks for dog and children as required.

'Can we go to the museum today, Mum?' said Gillian. 'It has lots of things about long ago. I love learning about history.'

'I like moo-see-ums too,' echoed Mike.

'Don't take Mega,' laughed Jason. 'If there are any bones there, she'll take them out and bury them.'

Mega barked. Had someone mentioned food? More food? No wonder dogs in the north looked so healthy. This was the way to live; good bones and plenty of exercise.

The museum was not a disappointment. The children learned about the things that their parents had been hearing from Mr Sinclair earlier that day.

It was, however, something else that captured their attention most of all. At one end of the museum was a building that reminded Gillian of a large industrial chimney. It was circular and wide at the bottom, narrowing as it rose to the top with a definite 'belly' about midway up.

'What is *that*?' murmured Jason in amazement.

'It's a broch,' answered the lady who was in charge of the museum. 'The people who lived here long ago were called Picts. The name means 'painted ones' and was given to them by the Romans who met them in battle, but didn't manage to defeat them.'

'In those days,' the lady went on, 'feuding and fighting were common. There was little of the law and order we have today. When invaders attacked the people, they would leave the huts in which they normally lived and hurry to the broch for safety.'

Pointing to the small entrance, she continued. 'This was the only way into the broch. A child or dog could walk in easily enough, or a cow or sheep, but a grown-up would have to bend down. Only one could enter at a time. When the people and their cattle were safely in the broch, one warrior with a spear could guard the entrance against a whole band of raiders.

'The broch had two walls, with an inside wall about twelve feet in from the one you can see. There was a stone stairway against the inside wall by which the people could climb to higher levels of safety between the two walls.'

'But how did the sheep and cows climb up?' asked Mike innocently.

'They didn't,' smiled the lady, 'they went right through the twelve foot entrance to the courtyard inside and were safe there.'

'How high was the broch?' asked Jason.

'It's hard to be sure but some were forty feet high, others maybe bigger. There's one only a few miles from here across the moor and it's still in good repair. I hope you'll be able to see it before you finish your holiday.'

The children thanked the museum curator and went outside again to play.

As they returned to the beach Jason remarked, 'I see it now. The broch wasn't home for the Picts, it was a refuge, just as a castle in medieval times. The people lived outside the castle and only entered across the drawbridge when the enemy attacked.'

The past was interesting, but more so the present, Mike thought as he sprinted towards the beach. The only castles he was interested in at the moment were sand castles.

'C'mon, Michelle,' he shouted, 'race you to the sea.'

Mike just beat his friend into the cool water and they splashed around in it for a time.

Then Michelle spotted a girl she had met the day before at the beach. She was about nine years old, the same age as her and, to Michelle's delight, had a small dinghy to play in. The girl was in the dinghy once more, so Michelle splashed across the beach to speak to her, leaving Mike to chase Mega.

'Will you help me to row the dinghy?' asked the girl. 'It's so difficult for one person.' Michelle nodded, jumped aboard and, taking one of the oars, paddled across the water. The girls had great fun.

'What's your name?' asked Michelle after a while.

'Margaret,' answered her new friend. 'What's yours?'

As Michelle answered, she became aware of the heightened sound of the wind, and also of agitated shouting from the beach. A glance behind told her that the dinghy had drifted far out to sea, and young though she was, Michelle realised that Margaret and herself were in real danger.

'Help!' she cried. 'Help us!'

Margaret began to cry. 'What will we do?' she asked.

Back on the shore, Jason and Gillian were nearly frantic with worry.

'Quick,' said Jason to his sister, 'go and fetch Dad.'

'What are you going to do?' she asked as she turned to run to the house.

'The only thing possible. I'm going to swim out to them.'

Grim-faced, Jason ran towards the sea which now seemed so hostile and threatening. Common sense told him there was nothing he could do.

The dinghy was too far out, but something within, something he did not understand, urged him forward. Michelle was like his own little sister and he could not give her up to the waves without a fight.

The cold water was lapping at his feet when a voice at his ear shouted firmly, 'Get back up the beach at once.'

A young man charged past him, plunged into the water and swam vigorously towards the drifting dinghy. Jason had seen the man minutes earlier at the far side of the beach where he had been doing some sort of exercises. How could he have covered all that ground so quickly?

The young man was a fast runner and a strong swimmer, and though the girls had seemed in serious danger, he quickly closed the gap until he reached them and began to pull the dinghy back to shore.

'Thank you, Lord,' prayed Jason, whose heart had been in his mouth through the whole frightening episode. 'Thank you, Lord, for sending that man.'

'Michelle.' It was Sue Reynolds. She had been on the way to the beach when Gillian had met her with the bad news. Frightened, she had rushed to the scene. Seeing the girls being dragged to safety brought home to her a sense of the seriousness of it all.

'Oh, thank you so much,' sobbed Sue as the rescuer brought the frightened, soaked pair ashore. She gripped the little girls to herself and wept gratefully.

'I know who you are,' exclaimed Jason, suddenly pointing to the young man who stood nearby, dripping wet and gasping from his wonderful efforts. 'You're Gordon Fraser, the athlete.'

The young man smiled quietly. 'I was training over near the rock pools when I realised that the girls were in trouble.'

'You must have run at some speed to get here in time,' remarked Paul Reynolds admiringly. He had just arrived with Margaret's anxious parents and shook the athlete's hand warmly.

'You should see him move, Dad, he's like a bullet,' added Jason admiringly.

Gordon Fraser was fast, and his strong build made him an ideal candidate for the 800 and 1500 metres.

Growing up in the northern moors and glens, he had none of the opportunities for training that many of his competitors had. Yet, he had proven as good as the best and had been chosen to represent his country on a number of occasions. Only two weeks before, he had beaten a field of international runners at Crystal Palace.

'You must come and have dinner with...' began Sue, but on turning she found that Gordon was already more than fifty yards away and picking up speed as he sprinted back to the far side of the beach.

'Speaking about food, Mum, I'm hungry,' said Gillian.

'Me too,' added Mike enthusiastically.

'I think we could all do with a meal,' said Paul. 'Let's go to the local restaurant. That'll give Mum a break.'

The idea was approved by all, especially by Sue who suddenly felt very tired after Michelle's frightening adventure.

After dinner the family went for a walk across the moor.

'There's the broch we heard about at the museum today,' cried Gillian.

'Will there be any Picts there?' asked little Mike.

'No, son,' said Paul with a gentle laugh. 'They died out hundreds of years ago.'

'Why does history have to be so old and long ago,' muttered Mike crossly.

'Mum,' said Gillian, 'imagine if there were Picts who had survived for centuries. Just like the Loch Ness Monster. Imagine if there were a Mr & Mrs Pict over a thousand years old still living in the broch.'

'There you go daydreaming again. There hasn't been anyone living in that broch for years.'

There was an air of finality and authority about Jason's words that was followed by a silence on the part of the other children.

'Let's go back to the house and play some games like Snakes and Ladders,' suggested Mum. She reckoned that they had all had enough outdoor adventure for one day.

The time of indoor games proved a big hit and helped Michelle and the others to forget their ordeal of the afternoon. Supper followed by evening prayers and soon they were tucked up in bed and fast asleep.

Jason didn't know how long he had been asleep, but something wet and fishlike was being thrust into his face and seemed determined to wake him. Slowly he realised that it was Mega's muzzle.

'Go to sleep, dog,' he mumbled and turned over on to his other side. The persistent animal trotted round the bed and prodded the reluctant Jason once again.

'What are you growling about, Mega?' muttered the weary boy as he blinked in the dawn light that was already penetrating the curtains of the bedroom.

Suddenly, remembering the experience the night before, he leapt out of bed and hurried to the window.

'It's them,' he gasped as his glance took in the group of night poachers, or whatever they were. The scene was almost exactly the same as the previous night.

'This time,' thought Jason, 'I'm going to follow them and find out where they're going and what they're up to.'

Hide-out in History

The figures were out of sight by the time Jason had slipped out of the house, warning to Mega to stay in the bedroom.

The poor animal's growling had given way to whining as it realised it was definitely going to miss out on something exciting.

Hurrying quietly across the moor, Jason soon picked up the trail. Dodging furtively between rocks and peat stacks, he followed the people in the direction of the caves. They did not go into the caves, however, but hurried on past.

'Where are they going?' wondered Jason. Then, as if by answer, the broch loomed into view.

'Surely they aren't going to hide fish in there. That doesn't make sense,' he mused. But it was to the broch they went and, with much grunting and panting, they manoeuvred the boxes they were carrying along the low entrance passageway until they were inside.

Jason drew near the door and was debating whether or not it was wise to investigate, when he heard the muffled sound of distant barking.

'Oh, no!' he moaned 'Mega's broken out. Any minute now and those thieves in there will hear her and be after the pair of us.'

Jason hurried back in the direction he had come, but by the time he had reached the caves Mega had caught up with him

'Be quiet, you bad dog,' he said angrily. "Bad dog" was a phrase seldom used by any of the Reynolds family, for Mega was immensely popular with all of them. It was a term of rebuke reserved for such unacceptable exploits as cat-chasing, slipper-tearing and refusing to come to heel when called, most of which Mega had outgrown. She was boisterous and full of fun as well as being an excellent watchdog, but she was never really bad.

Tail between her legs, Mega cowered quietly at Jason's feet. 'Come on, now, let's get home and keep quiet.' Keeping out of sight as best he could, Jason sprinted for home, his dog by his side. He didn't stop till he was safely through the window and had closed and locked it.

'That's how you got out, Mega. I forgot to close the kitchen window,' he said, fondling the animal's ears. Mega was glad that Jason no longer seemed angry with her and she settled down on the bedroom rug. Soon both boy and dog were fast asleep.

In the morning Jason was careful to say nothing about his dawn adventure until the other children were out of sight.

'Jason,' said his dad thoughtfully, 'I don't want you to speak about this to anyone until your mum and I have a chat.' The boy agreed and went out to play.

'I'm worried about Jason,' said his mum once he had gone.

'Exactly my own thought,' answered Paul.

'Shadowy figures carrying boxes of poached fish across a moor and hiding them in a broch! I can't believe it.'

'He always did have a lively imagination. Perhaps the sun's been a little too much for him. We certainly don't want the police hearing any more about it.'

'Let's pray,' said Sue, 'God can sort this whole thing out for us.'

A mother's concern had Sue Reynolds near to tears. What if her son was seeing things?

'Oh, Paul, let's cut the holiday short and go home. I'm frightened of what this place might be doing to the children.'

'Now that's enough,' smiled her husband taking her hand, 'haven't we just prayed? Do we trust our heavenly Father?'

'You're right, of course,' she replied, feeling relief as she let her faith sink more confidently into the God she had loved since childhood. It was ridiculous to pray without trusting. Paul hadn't been a Christian as long as she had, being converted in his early twenties. As Sue reminded herself so often, it was his faith that seemed more practical and more solid.

The door opened and Mike rushed in, followed by Michelle.

'Can we go for a walk with Gillian and Jason?' they chorused.

'Yes, but watch out crossing the road,' said Mum without thinking.

'There isn't a road on the moor, Mrs Reynolds,' said Michelle. 'There are no cars up here, apart from our own.'

Everyone laughed, for being so used to the city Sue had forgotten the benefit of living in a Highland glen.

The two relaxed as the family trooped off to explore whatever lay in their pathway. They might not have felt as at ease if they had seen where the walk was taking the four. It was Gillian who had wanted to look at the caves. They were interesting although not very deep. Michelle had a shock as she entered one cave and disturbed a sheep that had been resting there with its lamb. They nearly bowled the little girl over in their fright and she promptly retreated behind Mike.

Jason needed to use his loudest voice to restrain Mega who was all for giving chase after the disappearing sheep.

'That settles it, Mega, home you go,' said Jason, seizing her by the collar and marching her off to the house. Seeing his dad who had taken a basket outside to collect peat for the stove, Jason shouted from a distance, asking his dad to call Mega home. He watched as the Labrador bounded over the moor. What a great place this was for a dog.

By the time Jason got back to the caves he found that the others had moved on. Rounding a corner of the hill he saw them, and to his dismay they were running towards the broch.

'Stop! Stop! You mustn't go in there,' he shouted.

'Why not?' Gillian shouted back. 'You're just becoming a bossy boots!'

'But, I'm frightened,' said their brother, hurrying to catch up with them. He added in a lower voice that was less easily heard, 'It just might be dangerous.'

'But there aren't any Picts. You said so yourself,' said Mike, wondering why Jason didn't want them to have fun. Usually he was their leader in all their exploits.

'That's right,' smiled Gillian, hands on hips in defiance, 'you were quite sure. "No Picts" you said. "Not for hundreds of years." Why are you so frightened?'

'I'm not,' answered Jason firmly, aware that he wasn't being exactly truthful. 'I just don't want us getting hurt or lost or anything.'

He was too late, however, for Michelle was already running along the passageway with Mike after her. Jason hurried after them, with Gillian bringing up the rear. The entrance led into a large stone courtyard about fifty or sixty feet square.

'What a great place to play,' said Mike, his voice echoing eerily as it bounced off the high walls.

'Look over here,' said Gillian, 'this is the stone stairway we were told about at the museum.'

'I'll bet it goes all the way to the top,' said Jason, his excitement getting the better of his apprehension. He started to climb and quickly made his way from ground level to the first floor. He was just wondering what phrase the Picts used to describe the first floor of a broch when, to his horror, he heard angry voices coming from above.

Suddenly, a woman appeared at the top of the stairway. She was dressed in what looked like an animal skin, and behind her was a bearded man, dressed similarly.

They shouted at Jason in a language he did not understand. He opened his mouth to shout, but no words would come. Turning, he staggered down the stairs back to ground level.

'Lord, help me,' he prayed inwardly, gasping for breath. Suddenly he found his voice. 'Help!' he shouted, 'help!'

Gillian, Mike and Michelle were shocked to hear Jason's cries, and even more shocked to see him emerge ashen-face from the stairway.

'Get out, quick,' he gasped, 'there are strange people there.'

Gillian checked an urge to ask who the people were and what was strange about them. She realised her brother had received a terrific fright so, turning quickly, she shepherded the two younger children along the passage to the outer wall of the broch.

'Run for it,' shouted Jason, lending example to his words as he fled in the general direction of home. He had barely reached the caves when he was arrested by the sound of his name being shouted. It was Gillian.

'There's no one coming after us,' she shouted, her voice betraying both the surprise and irritation she felt. Jason had looked very convincing at the broch, but Gillian was beginning to wonder just what he was up to. Catching up with him she made it clear, in sisterly fashion, that she wanted to know what Jason had seen to make him so frightened.

'They were–like–Picts,' he stuttered. Gillian's surprise didn't lessen as he described what he had seen. At last, looking him straight in the eye, she asked, 'Are you sure you're not telling lies?'

The question struck fear into Jason's heart. His own sister had been there and she didn't believe him. How was anyone else likely to? His worst fears were realised when he arrived home and found that his mum and dad, though far more sympathetic than Gillian, obviously had doubts about his story.

'We can't go to the police, son,' said his father, 'because we don't have any evidence. Only you have seen these Picts and the strange people on the moor at night, and you're a complete stranger to the police here. They wouldn't believe you. I'm sure that what you saw was real to you, but...'

Paul Reynolds was interrupted by Jason as he burst into tears and ran outside. Not even his parents believed him.

'You'd better go after him, Paul,' said Sue, 'I'm going to start packing. There's something about this place that I don't like. We'll leave later today.'

Paul hurried after his son with a sinking heart. This was almost like a nightmare. At least Jason responded to his father's calls and came back to him. His eyes were swollen with crying.

'Dad,' he said, 'I know what I've seen.'

'Alright, Jason,' replied his father. 'I accept that I can't argue against your experience.

If you saw these people, you saw them. But, in that case, there's something very strange going on here and we're getting out of it. We're leaving Bettyhill today.'

Strange feelings mingled in Jason's mind. He was so relieved that his father seemed to believe him, and also that they were leaving a place that was so attractive on the outside and yet seemed to hold so sinister a secret. Yet at the same time he was sad to leave. To go now was to run away, and that couldn't be right for a Christian.

Father and son walked together to the beach. They were moving aimlessly along chatting, Paul with his arm comfortingly around the boy's shoulders. They scarcely noticed a man approaching them at speed.

'Hi there. Enjoying your holiday?'

The genial voice of Gordon Fraser took them both by surprise. Why he did not know, but Paul Reynolds found himself confiding in the fresh-faced young athlete. Together they told him the whole story as they walked along the shore.

The Secret of the Broch

Gordon Fraser shook his head as he listened.

'No, I don't think Jason's imagining these things. There's something very strange going on altogether.' Turning to Jason, he asked him, 'Has Mega wakened you up later on in the morning, say about four or five o'clock?'

Jason looked puzzled and shook his head.

'That means that Mega isn't hearing these poachers, or whoever they are, returning across the moor from the broch, after taking their catch in there. In fact, they probably go back to the village or to the pier by the way of the hill.'

'Oh, yes,' said Paul, 'I see, they come across the flat moor to the broch because it's easier to carry the fish that way.'

'But they go back over the hill when their hands are empty because it's safer than passing near the cottage,' Jason chipped in. 'Smart poachers.'

Gordon stopped in his tracks and looked at them. His normally bright features were heavy with concern.

'Unless I'm very much mistaken,' he said, 'these people aren't poachers, they're smugglers. I've lived here all my life. My parents and grandparents live here. We don't approve of organised poaching rings, but I can tell you they don't behave like this.'

'Then, you think Jason may have stumbled on something really big?' asked Paul.

'Really big, and maybe very nasty,' agreed Gordon, 'if these people are bringing three boxes of drugs per night into this country – three boxes so big it takes six men to carry them, then they could cause very serious trouble here.'

'What should we do, Gordon?' asked Jason, his enthusiasm for the hunt returning.

'I think we should have a quiet word with Sergeant Wallace. He's married to a cousin of mine and he'll give my little plan a chance.'

As they entered the police station they were greeted by Sergeant Wallace, who had a warm welcome for Gordon. 'When will you hear if you are chosen for the Olympic Team in London?' he asked.

'Soon, I expect,' replied the athlete with a smile. 'How's crime, or am I allowed to ask?'

'Och, we've had a street fight in South America, a gold bullion robbery in Amsterdam, fraud in London, and tourists who drive on the wrong side of the road in Sutherland,' replied Wallace, with a twinkle in his eye.

'Dad,' asked Jason in hushed tones, 'how can you drive on the wrong side of a single track road?'

'I heard that,' said the Sergeant with a laugh. 'You have your wits about you, son, that's for sure.'

The Sergeant listened patiently as Gordon explained what he had in mind.

His plan was simple. Sergeant Wallace would give the friends two hours to reach the broch, search it and report back. If they weren't back in that time, he would come along with a constable to find out why. That meant that if Gordon and Paul found themselves in difficulties at the broch, they could tell their captors that the police would be coming before the gang could escape.

The good thing about the plan was that it meant the police didn't have to get involved unless evidence could be found.

To Paul's surprise, Sergeant Wallace treated the whole thing very seriously.

'Crooks often choose obvious hiding places, trusting that nobody will bother to look there,' said the policeman.

As they left the police station, Jason asked his dad a question that had been puzzling him all along.

'What about the man and woman I saw in the broch, the Picts? Where do they fit into this?'

'They must be members of the gang who carried the boxes over the moor to the broch. I think that they dressed up to frighten you,' answered Paul.

'Yes, and to make you look silly,' added Gordon. 'After all, who is going to believe someone who thinks he sees Picts?'

That made perfect sense to Jason, who had almost begun to question the evidence of his own eyes. Jason's dad felt ashamed that he had ever doubted his son. It had seemed an extraordinary story.

'Can I come to the broch too?' asked Jason breathlessly.

'It isn't really safe…' began his father, but Gordon interrupted.

'If my hunch is right, these 'Picts' won't be there. The whole gang will have made good their escape and will be planning to come back tonight to move whatever it is they are hiding in the broch. If I'm right, then we'll be safe enough, and Jason could be a real help to us in our search.'

Jason was so glad to have found such a wise friend as Gordon, who seemed to understand just how much a boy loves adventure and doesn't want to miss any of the action. They soon arrived at the broch and made their way inside. Sergeant

Wallace had given them a flashlight to help them in their search. There was no one there, as Gordon had expected, and they were able to search the broch without interruption. They concentrated their attention on the area between the walls, with its different levels and stone stairway connecting them.

The three friends looked carefully for nearly an hour, covering all five levels and getting round most of the broch. They had found nothing and were beginning to despair when suddenly Jason stumbled, lost his balance and nearly fell down the stair from the fourth floor. Only quick action by Paul, who grabbed his arm, saved the boy from a very dangerous fall.

'Look, Dad!' cried Jason, recovering from his fright. 'No wonder I fell – the stone is loose.'

Quickly they pulled the stone out from the wall. By the light of the Sergeant's torch they could see that it was different from the others, a modern stone.

Shining the torch into the gap in the wall they saw something that made Jason gasp with surprise.

'Gordon, Gordon!' he cried, 'Up here, you were right enough. It's two costumes like those ancient Picts might have worn. Someone was trying to frighten us off.'

'That's great,' said Gordon, 'we're certainly on to something here. Paul, will you take these back to Sergeant Wallace and ask him to get a man here as soon as possible. Jason and I will keep looking. Maybe we'll find some clues about what the gang has stolen.'

Paul set off quickly to the police station. After replacing the stone Jason had fallen over, Gordon and the boy went back down to floor level to continue the search. Gordon reckoned that since smugglers' cargo was obviously heavy it would probably be hidden at ground level.

As Gordon searched again between the huge walls of the broch, Jason went out into the courtyard. The wide circular area would have held plenty of cattle at one time. It seemed strange to be standing in the same building where men and women had taken refuge centuries before – to be in the same place, and also to be in a measure of danger. Jason looked at the stones on the floor. Like the rest of the broch it had been very well put together, for the Picts had no special machinery to help them build.

As he was looking at the floor, it struck him that something was out of place. At first he hardly noticed, but the more he thought of it the more troubled he became. It was an iron ring on the ground, the sort of ring you would find on a trap door. Jason walked over to it and pulled. He felt some movement, but couldn't lift the heavy section of the floor.

'Gordon, look at this,' he called.

The athlete became excited as he saw it.

'This looks very interesting,' he said, pulling firmly on the ring. It was very heavy, but Gordon was strong and managed to raise it upright.

'Look at this. There are boxes in here,' Jason's excitement knew no bounds. Together the two of them heaved one box up out of the secret hiding place.

'Phew, what a weight,' gasped the boy.

'It certainly is,' agreed Gordon, 'this must weigh about one hundred pounds. Obviously this is what you saw being carried over the moor.'

'Isn't it strange to see a new box with a modern lock in an ancient broch,' observed Jason.

They waited until Sergeant Wallace arrived with two constables and watched excitedly as they smashed the lock to inspect the contents of the first box. When the lid was opened, gasps of amazement came from the gathered company, for the box was packed with gold bullion bars.

'The Amsterdam gold bullion,' said Sergeant Wallace tersely. 'How did it get here?'

'There are more boxes, Sarge,' said one of the constables, 'Here, Murdo, help me get this out.'

The two of them lifted the remaining boxes out. There were eleven of them, all filled with gold bars.

'There must be about a million pounds worth of gold here,' exclaimed Murdo.

'In that case there's more to come,' said Sergeant Wallace grimly. 'The thieves who stole this stuff from Amsterdam escaped with more than ten million pounds worth. Obviously the gang see this as a safe place to hide their loot and they'll probably plan to collect it when the hue and cry over the robbery has died down.'

They moved quickly, loading the boxes on to the trailer which PC Murdo Mackay had gone back to collect.

'I'll let headquarters know,' said Wallace to Gordon and Paul. 'They can handle it now. Indeed, Interpol will be brought in.'

Turning to Jason he said, 'You've done a wonderful job and you're a brave young man. Mum and Dad will be very proud of you.'

'It was really Mega who raised the alarm,' replied Jason. 'I would never have seen or heard these crooks but for her.'

'Mind you, there's one thing that bothers me about all this,' said the Sergeant thoughtfully. 'Why would these people be ready and prepared with ancient Pict clothing to scare you, Jason? It's almost as if they were expecting you. But how could they? How could they have known that you were on to them?'

'Hopefully we'll find that out when the police catch up with the gang,' said Gordon.

Police Headquarters informed Sergeant Wallace that they would be sending up a squad of detectives that evening to lie in wait near (and inside) the broch. Everything was to be hush-hush, and the news media were not to be told about the discovery so that the thieves wouldn't be warned off and escape the trap set by detectives.

Paul and Jason had agreed to say nothing to the other children for the time being, and Jason's mum knew how to keep a secret. Paul had mentioned to her briefly what had happened on their return to the police station with the gold bars.

That night Jason couldn't get to sleep. He waited near the window in his room, hoping to see the gang pass by once more in the dawn night. He was disappointed, however, for by three o'clock nobody had appeared. In sheer exhaustion he fell asleep, to be wakened in the morning by the noise of Mike and the barking of Mega as they ran in and out of the bedroom playing a game.

Slowly Jason realised that the dog hadn't wakened him during the early morning, presumably because she had not heard the sounds of the gang which had alerted her before. The boy's worst suspicions were confirmed when Sergeant Wallace called at the cottage during breakfast. The disappointment showed on his face.

Alone with Sue, Paul and Jason, he said, 'They never turned up. It may be that they planned to hide the rest of the gold somewhere else and left the district, but I suspect there was a tip-off. Are you sure you didn't tell anyone else?'

'No, we've seen nobody,' said Sue, 'apart from Mr Sinclair, the bailiff, and I just mentioned to him about the discovery of the gold. Naturally he promised to tell no one, and I'm sure he'll be used to keeping secrets. If you had been free to go to the broch the night before last you would have caught these thieves, Sergeant Wallace.'

'If I'd known they were in the area I would have made myself free. The first I knew of the matter was yesterday when your husband and son came to see me with Gordon.'

Sue Reynolds went white and began to fumble for words. 'But, we told Mr Sinclair and he said that he would inform you,' she said weakly.

'Never told me,' replied Wallace, his interest suddenly rising, 'and I was speaking to him two days ago. He was concerned that there were poachers operating up the river and wanted me to send a constable along. Actually, nothing happened.'

'But, Sergeant,' interrupted Sue, trembling, 'he told me yesterday that he had spoken to you two days ago about Jason seeing these people on the moor.'

There was a silence. All could see at once that someone was lying.

Peace Bay

'Train leaving in five minutes, sir,' replied the guard in answer to the angry question of the impatient man who kept glaring at his watch.

'Well, that's no good. It ought to have gone five minutes ago,' was the firm reply.

The guard shook his head. Travellers on the northern line weren't usually concerned about such a short delay. He couldn't know why Donald Sinclair was so anxious to be out of Thurso that morning, but he was soon to find out. Two burly police officers, whose last minute arrival in the station master's office had delayed the train's departure, strode down the aisle of the carriage from the guard's van.

'Donald Sinclair?' asked one of them abruptly. The colour drained from the bailiff's face. He could hardly believe it, the police were on to him already and the game was up. He had realised that Jason's inquisitiveness had changed everything. No more gold could be concealed in the broch and time was running out; he would need to escape quickly. He hadn't counted on the smartness of Sue and Paul Reynolds and the quick thinking of the police.

As he stepped off the train, the bailiff thought about how often he had caught poachers and of how he had despised them, how they deserved whatever sentence the sheriff passed on them in court. Now he had been caught, and his crime was far more serious than poaching. He found himself wondering how many years he would have to serve in prison.

What a fool he had been to listen to the smart-talking crook who had befriended him only two weeks ago. The man had involved him in the thieving racket with a promise of enough money to set him up for life. He would never need to work again the man had promised, and as proof had he not given him a first payment of £10,000? Donald Sinclair was not a Christian. Crime was just a lifestyle choice for him. He didn't care for God and God's laws. No, he had always prided himself in being too smart to be humble. How stupid he had been.

At the police headquarters Sinclair was cooperative, telling the police all he knew. Unfortunately, it was not very helpful, for they had guessed most of it already. The guard had told the bailiff all he needed to know to do his part of the job, but where they came from, or where the rest of the gold was, remained a mystery.

Investigation had established that the gold Gordon, Paul and Jason had discovered, was indeed part of the Amsterdam bullion which had been so dramatically stolen.

In the days that followed, the story was broadcast on TV and appeared in all the daily papers, but because Jason was a child, neither his name nor that of the family could be published. This turned out to be a blessing in disguise, for the gang were furious that their carefully prepared plans had been destroyed by a boy and his dog. Not only had they lost one million pounds worth of gold bars, but now it would be very difficult to hide the rest of the gold when coastguards and Interpol were on the alert. They were burning for revenge, but could not get at Jason.

Gordon Fraser was not so fortunate. Already something of a celebrity thanks to his exploits on the athletics track, he was now a household name through his part in the discovery of the gold bars.

One morning, while training on the deserted beach at Bettyhill the athlete scarcely noticed a speedboat bouncing on the waves in his direction. His concentration was soon interrupted by the sound of shouting. The pilot of the speedboat was calling to him and motioning for him to come over. Gordon jogged across obligingly.

'Excuse me,' began the man with a strong foreign accent, 'can you tell me where I would find John Mackay?'

Fraser laughed, 'I'm sure I can if you tell me which one you want. There are fourteen John Mackays here. It's a very common name in...'

Gordon's back had been to the speedboat, and he hadn't seen or heard the man's accomplice who had been lying low on the deck. It hadn't been difficult to creep up behind him, and a sharp crack on the back of the athlete's head was enough to leave him unconscious. The men quickly dragged him onto their speedboat, leaving as swiftly as they had come.

It was only when Gordon's parents and trainer reported him missing later that day that the police realised the seriousness of the situation. Detective Inspector Maclean of Highland Constabulary, who was in charge of the case, contacted the Reynolds. They were now at greater risk because the gang, bent on revenge, would almost certainly try to force Gordon Fraser to tell them the name of the family and where they were staying.

'We're moving you to a safe place so that even if the gang find out your names, they won't know where to look for you. There's no doubt about what their tactics will be now. Having kidnapped Gordon, they will try to get Jason or one of the other children and hold the authorities to ransom.'

'Do you mean they'll try to get back the million pounds using us as hostages?' asked Sue Reynolds in amazement.

'Yes, maybe even try to get safe passage abroad to spend the rest of the money too,' answered Inspector Maclean, adding grimly, 'they are desperate men and women who will stop at nothing.'

When Jason came to understand the danger Gordon Fraser was in, he went quietly to his room to pray.

'Oh, Lord,' he said, 'please look after Gordon. Help him to trust you and get the strength to go through whatever the gang do to him. And, Lord, please rescue him. Help the police to find him and capture the gang. Help them to get back all the money that was stolen. Thank you, Lord, you've promised to hear and answer prayer. May Gordon be able to run in the Olympics.'

Jason was learning to trust Christ at a deep level. He would never forget this holiday.

Later that day the family moved in a number of unmarked police cars to a place called Peace Bay. It was lovely and peaceful although, as Gillian reminded them, things had looked just as peaceful in the place from which they had come. Plain clothes policemen were keeping a discreet guard on the family without spoiling the holiday for the younger members.

Gillian found herself thinking a lot about Michelle. She liked the little girl and enjoyed having her with them on holiday. She fitted in well and was like a member of the family. Time and again that day, Gillian noticed Michelle and thought about her. Her mum had taught Gillian that when you find yourself thinking a lot about someone it may be that God is wanting you to pray for them.

Gillian prayed for her little friend. Then, even as she was praying, she sensed danger, not for Michelle, but for her parents. Sinclair, the bailiff, had known the little girl was from a different family. It might be that if the gang found out where the family was, one of them could be kidnapped. She told her mum who quickly informed the police. A message was flashed to the police in the area where Michelle's family lived, and at once they were removed to a place of safety.

The police action had not been a moment too soon, for that very evening two strange men were seen in the street watching Michelle's house. Before police could question them, they were gone. God's Holy Spirit had guided Gillian to give the warning just in time.

Gordon Fraser was being put under increasing pressure as the robber gang became more frustrated. Since his capture, Gordon had been in almost constant confusion and pain. He had awakened from unconsciousness following the blow on the head to find that he was blindfolded. He had no idea where he was, and could not understand what his captors were saying as they spoke in a foreign language. When he had protested at one point, demanding that his captors untie him and remove the blindfold, one had punched him in the face.

Gordon was finding time to think as he lay there. Where was he? At that moment the answer he wanted was spiritual as well as a geographic. Yes, he wanted to know where these men were holding him, but he also longed to know where he stood in relation to God. Gordon had grown up believing in God and seeing the importance of living a clean, upright life that showed respect for the teaching of the Bible.

As he listened to Sue and Paul Reynolds, Gordon had sensed that it was possible to know the Lord in a deeper and more personal way than he had ever done. Even young

Jason had the sort of faith that asked God to help in all sorts of things, big and small.

Right now Gordon was in big trouble. He needed God to be real to him as he so obviously was to the others.

Throughout the afternoon the young man came to realise just how serious his plight was. He was questioned closely by a man whose voice sounded hard and cruel. The man wanted to know where the Reynolds family were now and where they came from. Gordon was sure that this man and his gang meant to kill him and the whole Reynolds family.

The young athlete steadfastly refused to answer their questions in anything but the most general way, and, because this was unhelpful to the man, Gordon was repeatedly threatened and beaten. He was brave, but under cross-examination and due to his confused state, he let slip Michelle's surname which was an unusual one.

Quickly the gang had traced the few likely addresses Michelle's family could be living at and had arrived at the right house only hours too late to find them. Gordon's captors were furious and once again the athlete was beaten.

Gordon was in pain as he lay there, and he feared for his safety. However, he was more concerned for his parents, for he knew that they would be distressed by his disappearance. Nevertheless, there was a quiet satisfaction in seeing the gang's plans so obviously frustrated. Somehow it was as if God's hand was very much in control of the whole situation and all would be well.

The Map

'Mum, I'm bored,' said Gillian Reynolds.

'Me too,' added Jason.

Sue could hardly believe it. Hadn't they had enough danger and adventure to keep them happy for years to come, or at least until the end of the holidays?

'Mum, can we climb the rocks and look for birds' eggs?' asked Jason.

'You certainly may not,' chipped in his dad. 'Those rocks are steep and dangerous.'

'Then, at least let's climb that hill,' said Gillian, pointing out of the cottage window to the large grassy slope that swept upwards from the beach.

'That should be safe enough, Paul,' suggested Sue.

'Fine,' replied Dad, 'but be careful.'

'We will, Dad,' they promised, ' can we take the binoculars?' Dad nodded.

True Gold

The hill was steeper than the children had expected and they were panting by the time they reached the top. The beautiful view out across the Atlantic Ocean made their efforts worthwhile, however, and they sat for nearly half an hour looking at the sea, the islands in the distance, and the birds who inhabited the nearby rocks.

'Pity Dad won't let us go over to those rocks. They look ace,' said Jason longingly.

'Let's go over in the other direction, away from them,' said his sister, who was beginning to see the wisdom in their parents' refusal. Those rocks certainly looked dangerous to her.

To their surprise, the broad hill sheltered another bay almost directly behind the one where their new hideaway cottage was situated. It, too, was beautiful.

'That's a brilliant boat anchored down there in the bay,' gasped Jason. 'Let's have a look with the binoculars.'

The yacht certainly was impressive, and Jason's scrutiny took in the bows and bridge, the mast and stern.

Suddenly a distant whirring sound caused the boy to swing the binoculars out to sea. A speedboat was making its way towards the bay.

'I'd love to go out on the speedboat,' said Gillian longingly as she took the binoculars.

She was turning to walk back over the hill when Jason hissed at her. 'Gillian, wait! Get down! Give me the binoculars quickly.'

The boy had seen something dramatic. As Gillian looked back down to the yacht she saw a figure she knew well, even though he was blindfolded.

'It's Gordon,' she gasped

'Keep quiet, and keep down,' urged her brother.

Gordon Fraser had been brought out from the yacht by two men. They had obviously intended to put him on board the speedboat, but after a discussion between the two men and those on board the smaller boat, Gordon was taken back into the yacht.

'The Picts,' said Jason excitedly.

'What?' replied his sister.

'It's the Picts. That man and woman from the speedboat. They're the people I saw in the broch. They were dressed in skins, but I would recognise them anywhere.'

The speedboat pulled away sharply, and Jason watched excitedly through the binoculars.

'One of the two men who were on board the yacht is going away with the boat! If my reckoning is correct there's only one man left on board the yacht guarding Gordon.'

'If we could get Dad to distract the man, we could get on board and set Gordon free,' suggested Gillian.

Jason shook his head. 'You know what grown-ups are like. As soon as you cut them in on something they take over and send you to bed or something. Dad wouldn't allow us to get involved in anything like this. He would think it too dangerous.'

'Then we need someone else to distract the man,' said Gillian. 'But who?'

As she saw her brother looking very pointedly at her, she began to protest. 'I can't go down there. If that man catches me I'll get blindfolded too.'

'He needn't catch you if you do what I say. Wait here until I come back, then I'll explain.'

'Where are you going?' asked his sister nervously. 'Jason, you're not heading down there?'

'Try to be quiet,' hissed her brother over his shoulder. 'I'll be back in a few minutes.'

Jason took off down the hill, taking care to keep out of sight as best he could. Soon he was on the beach near the rocks. He slipped into the water and silently waded out to the yacht. There was a rope ladder hanging over the side, and climbing stealthily upwards, he reached the deck. A furtive glance through a cabin window was enough to tell him that Gordon was tied up and that one of the crooks was guarding him.

Away from the window, Jason crouched down and listened. The yacht's radio was not in use. His plan might just work. Edging his way along the side of the cabin, he cleverly disconnected the upright aerial from its fixture, immobilising the radio. Quietly he climbed over the side of the boat and down the rope ladder. As he waded back to shore, he kept the aerial clear of the water, then swiftly carried it back up the hill to Gillian.

'That was awesome,' she said with unusual admiration and not a little concern. 'But what if they'd caught you?'

'That's why I needed you to pray for me,' he answered, 'and now I'll need to pray for you.'

'What do you mean?' asked Gillian, turning slightly pale.

'I want you to keep this aerial here while I go back to the shore and find a hiding place. From there I'll throw stones at the cabin and get the guard to come out and investigate. When he comes out, you make a noise and wave the aerial. Hopefully he'll chase you.'

'What do you mean "hopefully he'll chase me?" What if he catches me?' demanded Gillian indignantly. She wasn't at all keen on this brotherly brainwave.

'He won't. You have a good start on him.'

'But Jason, I'm scared!' wailed Gillian.

'Look!' said her brother getting more and more exasperated. 'Do you want to help Gordon or not?'

'Of course I do,' sniffed Gillian, 'but...'

'That settles it then,' Jason broke in determinedly. 'Just wait until I get down to the rocks, then I'll throw those stones.'

Gillian wanted to protest, but it was too late. Jason had set off towards the rocks and she could only hide the binoculars, then watch and wait.

Jason quickly found a hiding place, then picked up a stone and threw it at the yacht. He missed the target and tried again. This time the stone hit the cabin door squarely with a resounding bang.

The door swung open to reveal the angry features of the crook. His anger turned to surprise when he saw that no one was standing there.

'This is it,' gulped Gillian.

She jumped up, waving the aerial wildly above her head and shouted at the criminal. 'Hey, you down there. Here's your aerial. If you want it, come and get it.'

The man roared something in his own language which Gillian was glad she didn't understand. In his rage the crook was already rushing towards the rope ladder. He needed the aerial.

'Jason will be pleased,' thought Gillian, suddenly relishing the excitement of this dangerous exploit.

She waited as the man waded through the water and ran across the beach, shouting furiously as he advanced towards her. He was beginning to climb the hill when Gillian noticed Jason sneaking out from behind a rock and slipping into the water to make his way towards the cabin.

Gillian's moment of triumph was short-lived, for looking round towards the man again, she saw to her horror that he was gaining on her rapidly.

Jason reached the rope ladder and looked quickly in Gillian's direction. She had stopped to pick something up, but was soon racing towards the top of the hill with the criminal in hot pursuit. Jason watched anxiously. There was a long, straight stretch before she could reach the hill leading down to the bay where her family were hiding.

'Lord, please keep her safe. Don't let him catch her,' he breathed, starting to climb the ladder.

Gillian was running out of breath, but kept going as fast as she could. The man's angry voice was getting louder and louder. She dropped the aerial, hoping that this would distract the crook, but although he picked it up, he quickly came after her again. This child had appeared out of nowhere and he was determined to find out who she was and how much she knew.

It was no good. She realised that she was going to be caught at any moment and turned to face her pursuer. Now there was nothing else for it. She had kept this in hand for emergencies.

As the evil-looking man reached out to grab her, Gillian flung a handful of sandy earth into his face. Then, turning round, she fled as fast as her legs would carry her.

The crook was taken completely by surprise. Temporarily blinded he spluttered and staggered around helplessly until his eyes cleared. This distracted him for so long that Jason had time to release Gordon. He was ready to lead Gordon off the boat to the far side of the beach, but the athlete shook his head.

'If we leave this yacht here, He'll escape on it, or at least send a radio message to the gang. Let's sail the yacht round to the next bay, where your folks are, and to the detectives. That way the man will be stranded here and the gang will be none the wiser.'

The angry gang member had barely cleared the burning sand from his eyes when he heard the engine of the yacht starting up. Shouting wildly he sprinted back down the hill in a desperate attempt to stop the friends. He hauled out a revolver and fired repeatedly until each chamber was empty, but the yacht was already out of range and moving steadily out of his vision. What would his boss say now? More importantly, what would his boss do now?

'Where did you learn to handle a boat so well?' asked Jason, full of admiration for Gordon Fraser's nautical skill.

'When you grow up in a coastal village you have many opportunities to sail and steer a boat,' he replied, adding, 'This one certainly is a beauty.'

Jason agreed, his eyes taking in the luxury and splendour of his surroundings. As he looked around, his eyes suddenly alighted on something interesting. 'Look at this,' he cried excitedly. 'It's a map.' He brought it to Gordon so that he could look at it.

'It's a map of the north and north-west coasts of Scotland,' observed the athlete, 'Hello, what's this?' There were three spots marked in red ink.

'One of them is obviously the bay where the yacht was anchored,' said Jason. 'Isn't it amazing that of all the bays, inlets and sea-lochs in the north west of Scotland, they should have picked the one next to where we were being hidden.'

Gordon looked at the youngster. 'That wasn't a coincidence, was it?'

Jason shook his head, 'No, it was the plan of God to catch these crooks.'

'And to answer our prayers,' said Gordon. 'I did a lot of thinking and praying when I was tied up on board that yacht. I realised just how much I need God to be in charge of my life.'

They had arrived at the shore of Peace Bay to the amazement of Jason's parents and the detectives, who had placed themselves on alert as soon as they had seen the boat approaching. At that moment, a yell from the hill above the bay announced the arrival of Gillian.

The detectives were surprised by the children's adventure, for they hadn't even missed them as they climbed over the hill. After reporting the news to their base and assuring that a patrol boat would be on its way directly, both men set off over the hill to apprehend the stranded gangster.

'Dad, look at this,' said Jason. 'It's a map of this area and there are red marks on it.'

'We should have shown it to the detectives,' said Gordon, 'but they were off before I remembered.'

'This red mark is the bay where Gordon was held prisoner,' began Jason.

'Until you two came and rescued me,' said the young man giving them a hug.

'Then this mark here,' said Paul Reynolds, pointing to the second one, must be the broch where the gold bars were hidden. So what about this third mark? It's not on land at all, but out in the Atlantic Ocean off the north coast.'

'Wait a minute,' interjected Gordon excitedly, 'there is land there – a small island called Eilean nan Ron.'

'That must be Treasure Island,' said Mike, to a chorus of laughs from the others.

'Mike,' cried Gillian, 'I think you're right. It is treasure island. It's where the gang have hidden the rest of the money.'

'Well, you could be right,' agreed Gordon Fraser. 'Eilean nan Ron was inhabited until 1937 when the last of the people came to the mainland to live. There are about a dozen old houses in a state of disrepair. It would be easy to hide money there, and until we exposed what they were doing, the gang could have been hiding out there themselves. During the time I was their prisoner, though, most of them were on board the yacht almost all the time.'

When the detectives returned with their prisoner in handcuffs, Gordon and Paul showed them the map and further discussions took place. The patrol boat arrived with Detective Inspector Maclean on board, and he and the team quickly drew up plans. They would search the yacht thoroughly, both for clues and as a precaution in case it was wired up for explosives. If all was well, they would sail it back to its original anchorage in the neighbouring bay. Only this time it would be full of armed police, backed up by a unit on the shore.

'They are a dangerous bunch,' Maclean confided to Gordon and the Reynolds family.

'The one we, or rather you, picked up has a long record of violent crime, including manslaughter.'

Sue Reynolds felt cold shivers run down her back. To think her children had been that close to a killer. 'O, dear Lord, thank you for your mercy in keeping them safe,' she said almost involuntarily.

'Amen to that,' added Maclean. 'If only people knew how often God intervenes to help people in need, they would be more ready to trust him with their lives.'

The Inspector then turned to Gordon, 'I don't expect you'll have heard the radio today?'

'Hardly,' laughed the tall young man, 'there hasn't been time. Any good programmes?'

'Yes, the news would have interested you. You've been chosen for the British Olympic Team. You're running the 800 and 1500 metres in London if we can get you out of here in time.'

The Boat Comes In

Detective Inspector Maclean was delighted at the progress made in the bullion robbery case. He had quietly prayed that God would provide the key to unlock the door of this mystery and it had happened, even before the British public had become aware of the drama unfolding on the northern shores of the country.

It was remarkable that the announcement of Gordon Fraser's selection for the Olympic Team should have been made while the athlete was still being held captive by the robber gang. The sporting authorities had known nothing of his plight.

Delighted though he was, Maclean was anxious to catch the gang before they realised what was happening and had scattered to the safety of some foreign country or other. He was sure that they would try to return to the yacht in the western bay, but he also felt that if the rest of the gold bars were hidden on Eilean nan Ron they would be bound to call there. Maclean therefore decided to alert the coastguards both to the west, at Cape Wrath, and to the east, at Thurso, so that the thieves would find no hole in the net to slip through. So much depended on the gang not knowing that their hostage had been rescued.

Night fell and Maclean waited patiently on the hill above the bay. Just after midnight the faint sound of a distant engine could be heard, followed by the headlights of a speedboat. The police officers both on the hillside and the yacht waited patiently. The boat drew nearer. The engine cut out some distance from shore.

Maclean waited, heart in mouth. Was there some pre-arranged signal of flashing lights needed, without which the speedboat would not come into the bay? The waters lapped quietly. The Detective Inspector waited. If that speedboat turned and fled now, there would be no alternative but to give chase and be prepared to turn all the fire-power in the police armoury upon this band of dangerous international crooks.

Time passed. Maclean prayed that they would come in. Slowly, almost grudgingly, the speedboat drifted to the shore. Angry, frustrated voices from the speedboat hailed the dimly-lit cabin of the yacht.

At last the speedboat was alongside and one member of the gang climbed aboard the yacht. Suddenly the bay was a blaze of light. Policemen were everywhere. Two shots rang out from the high-power rifles, smashing the speedboat engine and making a quick escape impossible.

The gang were stunned. They never imagined that people could possibly have found their hideaway, and so quickly. They were arrested, cautioned and bundled aboard a police launch which had been anchored in the darkness of Peace Bay. In all there were six arrests, four men and two women.

The gang leader, a notorious crook called Der Antieken, was furious.

'You have no right to arrest law-abiding citizens in this way. When we get to Inverness you will look very foolish in front of the Sheriff.'

The Detective Inspector guffawed in the man's face. 'The Sheriff,' he barked. 'Do you imagine your case will be dealt with by a Sheriff Court? No, my man. It'll be the High Court in Edinburgh for you.'

Der Antieken sat down sulkily. Obviously this was no simple country bobby, unaware of international crime. Looking around suddenly, the gang leader jumped to his feet. 'This isn't the way to Edinburgh. It's to the south.'

'Och, we're just taking a wee trip along the north coast, past an island that used to be inhabited. It's called Eilean nan Ron. You might know about it. It's marked here on your map.'

As Maclean brought out the map that Jason and Gordon had found on the yacht, Der Antieken went pale. The crooks argued together in their own language.

'Now let me make it simple for you,' Maclean said, looking straight at Der Antieken, 'the game is up. If you tell us where you've hidden the £9,000,000 it might influence the judge when he comes to pass sentence. He might make it a bit lighter on you. Mind you, I can't promise anything.'

The gang leader scoffed at the detective. 'You're bluffing. We don't know anything about gold bars. We are on a fishing holiday. Wait till my lawyer gets hold of you.'

'Who said anything about gold bars? I just mentioned £9,000,000,' replied the Inspector, a look of triumph on his face. Der Antieken scowled. He had given himself away once more.

One of the gang members turned to his boss and spoke haltingly in their own language. There was fear on his face. Der Antieken argued and glowered threateningly at him, but the anxious man turned to the police chief and said in English, 'I'll show you where the gold is hidden.'

The boxes of bullion had been heavy and the gang had decided to hide them near the little harbour on the island rather than carry them up the stairway that led to the desolate houses. The gold was loaded onto the yacht, which was being brought back to the harbour at Thurso. Before the night was out both criminals and their loot were safely locked away.

When the story broke the next day, it commanded the headlines in newspaper and on television. Now that the gang were in custody it was safe to reveal Jason's name and to interview the whole family. People everywhere were stunned to think of an international gang of bullion robbers using an ancient broch, distant bays and islands as if they were twentieth century treasure islands and modern day smugglers' coves.

Most of all, the British public were amazed to hear that this dangerous gang had been brought to justice principally through the cleverness of a boy and his dog, and the courage of a young athlete.

Jason and Gordon, not to mention Mega, found that they were heroes overnight. All sorts of people wanted to talk to them and hear them speak of their adventures, but because the case against Der Antieken and his gang had still to come to court, there was very little that they could say.

Both Gordon and Jason made it clear how much the Lord Jesus Christ mattered to them and how they found God drawing very close to help them when things were specially hard or dangerous. As Jason put it to one man who interviewed him on television, 'If I was brave, it was God who made me brave.'

For Gordon Fraser there was a new pressure to face, that of running in the Olympic Games. He had been chosen to represent Britain in races where he would be facing the finest runners in the world, representing many different countries. The few days in captivity had set his training schedule back quite a bit, and he had hardly made up for lost time when he had to leave for London with the British team.

Some sports writers had never been very keen on Gordon for the Olympic Team. They were unsure of his training methods and felt he might not fit in with the rest of the team. These doubts and reservations had been expressed even more forcibly since the news of his capture and the ordeal he had suffered. It wasn't that they didn't respect or like Gordon. They just weren't used to somebody like him.

Whatever anyone else might think, one family who were sure that Gordon would do well were the Reynolds. Furthermore, they were going to be in London cheering him on. This special treat had been given to them as a reward by the bank from which the bullion had been stolen. It was a perfect holiday and both parents and children were looking forward to it. 'Will there be lots of ice cream?' Mike kept asking.

'And fizzy drinks?' queried Michelle.

'Yes, oh, yes,' laughed Gillian, 'and if you stop guzzling long enough you might see some people running races.'

When the family arrived in the capital they found that it was all they had hoped for. It was a beautiful city, and the people were very friendly to the thousands of visitors from different parts of the world.

The opening ceremony was spectacular as athletes from over a hundred nations marched behind their national flag, while the massed bands played the different national anthems. Then followed the special gymnastic displays, which had kept the children enthralled. Finally, there was that special moment when the Olympic Torch was carried into the stadium by a runner who lit the flame that would burn throughout the time of the games.

It was all marvellous, but one very special moment came for the Reynolds family when the British team marched past. They were cheered wildly by the people who had come to the games from all over the United Kingdom.

'Where's Gordon, Mum? I can't see him,' said Jason.

'There he is, at the end of the second row of men,' she answered. Jason recognised him and shouted wildly.

When at last the ceremony was all over the children returned with their mum and dad to have dinner in the lovely hotel the bank had booked them into.

'I think I'm going to enjoy this holiday,' said Gillian. 'There are just so many things to see, and I can't wait to cheer for Gordon as he wins those races.'

'Oh, now, Miss Dreamer, it won't be quite as simple as that. Gordon is good, but he will be competing against the best,' said Dad.

'We must pray for him,' piped up Mike. 'That way he'll win.'

'Certainly we must pray for Gordon and we should do that now before you all go off to bed,' replied Mum, 'but we can't pray for him to win. We must pray that Gordon will be able to do his best. You see, he will be nervous knowing that he is to run against these great athletes, and knowing that the so-called experts don't expect him to win.'

'That's right,' said Jason, 'I read a newspaper that's on sale here and it said it was very unlikely that any of our men will get anything better than a bronze medal in either the 800 metres or the 1500 metres.'

'Often in sport a game or race is won and lost before it's even started,' agreed Dad, 'because the competitors have come to believe how they will perform even before they get on to the field or track.'

'We must pray that God will help Gordon to forget all the things men say or think and just look to Christ to help him do his best,' said Mum. 'Listen to this passage in the New Testament, from Hebrews 12:1-2 "…let us lay aside every weight, and the sin that clings so closely and let us run with patience the race that is set before us, looking unto Jesus, the author and finisher of our faith…"'

'Does that mean we have to run a race too, Auntie Sue?' asked Michelle. Mike laughed at the idea, but his mum nodded.

'Yes, Michelle,' she answered. 'Our race is different. It's really how we live. Athletes like Gordon have to train and watch their diet so that they don't become overweight, because that would hinder them as runners. With us it's different. The thing that holds us back is having a whole lot of other ambitions that hinder us from that all important thing – following Jesus.'

'Yes,' added Paul, 'and especially sin. That means things we say or think or do that displease our Lord. We can't live for him properly if we're doing these things.'

'I suppose,' said Gillian sadly, 'that includes having nasty feelings towards people. I don't like one of the girls at school because she says bad things about me and other Christians and gets others to laugh at us.'

Mum felt sad for Gillian, but she was firm as well as kind with her.

'You must forgive that girl. If you are angry with her you can't please Jesus. You are slowing yourself down as his follower. Let's ask the Lord to help you with this problem, and to help all of us to be good Christians.'

'And let's not forget to pray for Gordon that he'll be able to do his best,' added Jason.

One by one, all of them prayed. They asked God to forgive wrong things in their lives and to help them do the right thing. Each of them prayed for Gordon, thanking God for the good times they had already had with him. They asked that he might run his races without fear of losing, and might enjoy this special experience of competing in the Olympics.

Their prayers at an end, the children went off to bed. They were tired. They had had a wonderful day but needed their rest. Soon they were asleep and Sue and Paul Reynolds could relax quietly and talk together of all the things that had happened over those few weeks. It all seemed too amazing to be true. Before long they were also asleep.

One person who had been finding it extremely hard to sleep was Gordon Fraser.

In the British team headquarters he had already had two nights of broken rest due to nightmares as a result of his capture. He wasn't a nervous person, but seemed unable to control the problem. He made up his mind that if this continued he would have to speak to the team doctor. That night, however, he settled down and slept like a log.

Note from a Poison Pen

'Right, lads, that's enough for this morning.' The rasping voice of Tim Horsfell was music in the ears of the British 800 and 1500 metre runners. Tim was team coach for these middle distance runners and he knew just how to bring the best out of the athletes without over-extending them.

'Gordon,' the coach called, beckoning the young Scot towards him.

'I'm glad to see you held up well in training today. I sensed you were struggling a bit yesterday and the day before, but you've settled fine. I was afraid you might have to call off the heat for the 800 metres. I suppose it must have been the tension of these past weeks.'

Gordon nodded. He hadn't been aware that the coach could see so clearly how he was feeling. Jogging off for a shower,

Gordon whispered a prayer. 'Thank you, Lord for giving me the rest I needed so much. Help me with my last minute preparation.'

Apart from some more light training and tactical talks, Gordon was able to relax for the rest of the day. Once again he slept well, rising the next morning full of anticipation for the race he would run that day. There were two heats and the fastest runners in each would qualify.

Gordon only needed to look at the athletes he would be competing against to know his task was going to be difficult. There was Oltavelli of Italy, Seznitsm of Russia and MacGregor of Canada, to mention but a few. In fact, they all looked winners to Gordon, who was tempted to feel that he would never manage to qualify for the final. Again he found himself praying, 'Lord, help me to do my best.'

The starter's pistol fired and the race was under way. Seznitsm went to the front quickly and set a cracking pace, faster than Gordon had expected. The temptation to throw tactics to the wind and sprint after the Russian was great, but he resisted it and quickened his pace just enough to stay in touch with the leaders.

The bell rang at the end of the first lap indicating that there was only one lap to go. Gordon was lying about eighth.

Momentarily, he glanced behind and discovered to his surprise that a considerable gap had opened up between the first eight and the others.

The pace didn't slacken over the second lap and Gordon was beginning to feel the strain. Two hundred metres from home there were still seven runners in front of him.

Making a mighty effort he moved out to overtake two of them. There were less than one hundred metres to go and he was lying sixth. Gritting his teeth he threw everything into one last desperate effort, which brought him up into the pack of five who crossed the finishing line almost together.

The qualifying time was remarkably fast and Gordon, who had officially been fourth equal, was certain to qualify. The remaining heat was also run in excellent time and there were about an equal number of qualifiers from it, including another British runner, Sam Lewis, from London.

'You did very well, lads,' said Tim Horsfell encouragingly. 'It was a really fast field and the best time this year was by Bob Givens of the United States in that second heat. It should be a great final and you can both be up there amongst the medals. That's what the folks back home will be hoping to see.'

Gordon felt good that evening as he returned to his hotel room. He had seen a number of track and field events and enjoyed them all. Qualifying for the final of the 800 metres made it all that much better.

But he was in for a rude awakening when he opened the door of his room. A note had been pushed under the door. It said simply, 'You will not return home alive.'

As Gordon read those words it seemed as if there were lights flashing around his eyes. For a few minutes he could hardly think straight. Surely this must be the work of the bullion gang, but they were in jail. No athlete would descend to this sort of behaviour, or would he? Maybe other members of the British squad had received similar notes.

Gordon made his way downstairs to find Tim Horsfell. The coach was stunned. 'I've heard this kind of thing happen to sportsmen, but I've never encountered it myself before. We'll mention this to our Secretary and I imagine he'll inform the police. Try not to let it bother you. It's probably a crank.'

Gordon smiled weakly, 'The trouble is that just occasionally one of these cranks does something dangerous.' Seeing Tim's concern, he added, 'Don't worry, Coach, I haven't come all this way to quit. I'll see it through.'

'I know you will, son,' replied the coach, 'Meanwhile we will do all we can to sort this problem out.'

Gordon didn't sleep well that night, and his worries built up again when he found a letter waiting for him.

'There was no stamp on this letter, sir,' explained the porter. 'It was handed in this morning.'

The young athlete opened the letter nervously, but to his delight it was from the Reynolds family. They were congratulating him on his wonderful performance in qualifying for the final of the 800 metres, and assuring him of their prayers for the remainder of the races.

This letter was not only welcome, but to Gordon it was as if God was speaking through this lovely family to reassure him. Eagerly he checked the top of the letter. Sure enough, the Reynolds address was there. A quick word with Tim Horsfell confirmed that the athletes were free later that afternoon, and he telephoned the Reynolds' hotel to arrange a get-together with them later that day.

The encouragement the letter had given Gordon helped him with the day's training. There were only two full days' work-out before the heats for the 1500 metres, and he needed to use every hour on track to best advantage.

'You're in peak condition, lad, and your mental attitude is excellent,' beamed Tim Horsfell as Gordon finished training for the day. Once again the coach had done his work superbly. Turning to the whole squad he reminded them, 'You have three hours until dinner. Relax and take it easy.'

None of the runners needed a second invitation to do that, for they were all beginning to feel very tired.

When Gordon arrived at the hotel where the Reynolds were staying he received a warm welcome from the family. He couldn't help noticing what a wonderful thing true Christian fellowship was. He had only known this family for a few weeks, and, in a sense they had brought such turmoil into his life. Yet, because they had shared the gospel of Jesus Christ with him, he had found the greatest blessing in life, and now the whole family were like brothers and sisters to him.

Once the children had gone to the hotel swimming pool, Gordon told Paul about the threatening note he had received the previous evening.

'It could be a crank,' agreed Paul, 'but I don't think so. Inspector Maclean is a shrewd man and he feels sure they haven't caught all the gang yet. He thinks that there's at least one loose. If so, he'll be out for revenge.'

'Have you a list of the names of other competitors in the 800 metres, or any other information that would tie any of them to the gang?'

Gordon shook his head. Paul brightened up, 'It will be very difficult for anyone to get at you on the track without showing themselves and being caught.'

'And most important of all,' added Sue, 'the Lord is with you all the time. Remember this promise: "Many are the afflictions of the person who is right with God, but the Lord delivers him out of them all" (Psalm 34:19).'

'New Christians often find themselves faced with very difficult problems, but as they learn to trust God through them, they grow stronger in their faith and become better able to help other people later on.'

'Yes,' observed Paul, 'that's right. It's just as it is put in the New Testament: "No discipline (or testing) is pleasant, but painful. Yet afterwards it brings us the peace of having drawn nearer to God" (Hebrews 12:11).'

Paul went on, 'You've certainly been a great encouragement to us, Gordon. Our faith in Christ has grown as we have seen you developing as a Christian. You can be sure of our prayers.'

Gordon thanked them and, after they had prayed together, he went to the pool to see the children before leaving.

There were no further poison pen notes that night or the next, and Gordon rose on the morning of the heat with his mind clear and as prepared as possible. His favourite race was the 800 metres, but he had been improving as a 1500 metre runner and had become one of the fastest in Britain over that distance. Once again he faced a star-studded field and realised that he would have to be at his best to qualify.

The pace over the first lap was not too fast, but it had quickened considerably by the end of the second, and Gordon had to increase his speed to keep in touch with the leaders. If he had hoped the pressure would ease as the runners entered the third lap he was in for a disappointment. Aboukar of Saudi Arabia was setting the pace and he stepped it up so that the young Briton, along with the others, was battling to keep in touch with the frontrunners.

By the time the bell had signalled the last lap, Gordon was ten yards behind the pack of seven leaders, and realised that if he was going to qualify for the final he would need to make a powerful effort and he would need to make it now. Gritting his teeth and lengthening his stride he tore after the disappearing pack.

Slowly, painfully slowly, he gained on them. The slogging of the past year and especially the training of the last few days was paying off.

As he came into the home strait he was level with the Ethiopian and German runners in fifth and sixth places, and over the last hundred metres he overtook the American and Czech athletes just ahead of them. His tremendous effort had brought him third place and certain qualification for the final.

Tim Horsfell and some of the British runners gathered round to congratulate him. They were delighted that at least one British runner had qualified for the final.

'That was magnificent, Gordon. It was a fast pace and to catch them after slipping back was tremendous.'

'There are one or two things I need to work at,' said Gordon, 'such as my start and my stride. I found myself in trouble early on in each of these races and had to fight to get back at the end.'

Tim Horsfell nodded. 'There are a few things we can look at in training tomorrow that would help. I'm confident that you'll do well. I noticed one or two of those world class athletes looking at you after the race. They know they'll have their work cut out to beat you.'

After answering reporters' questions, the British runners returned to their hotel. It was Friday and the two finals would not take place until the Wednesday and Saturday of the following week, giving each of them time to improve their performance.

When he reached his room, Gordon thanked God for helping him to run so well. He was sure it was not only the long spells of training and the wise coaching which were improving his ability. It was also the strength and confidence the Lord was giving him and the peace of mind he had in spite of the anonymous note.

As he sat at dinner with the team that evening, Gordon was approached by a waiter who said that there was a telephone call for him. He made his way to the desk and picked up the receiver.

'Hello, Gordon Fraser here.'

There was silence at the other end of the line.

'Hello... Hello.'

A hard, chilling voice answered. 'The Picts are not all dead.'

'What?' gasped Gordon, 'Wha' ...what do you mean?'

But the voice only repeated the words: 'The Picts are not all dead.' Then the caller hung up.

Gordon thought about the voice he had just heard. Though it was muffled and indistinguishable the tones were hard and cruel. It was a man's voice, but that was all that could be said with certainty.

'Are you alright, sir?' asked the clerk at the desk.

'What? Oh, yes,' replied Gordon, who was feeling anything but alright. His immediate reaction was to telephone the Reynolds, but he realised that he could not keep doing this. Instead he turned to God. 'Lord, help me through this,' he prayed. 'I cannot see these people but you can and you can restrain them.'

Gordon thought about his prayer and remembered God's promise to give what his people needed in answer to prayer. He returned to the dinner table composed and at ease. No one sensed that he had just received a disturbing phone call.

Three of the following four days were filled with training. Sunday was free and Gordon went to a church service in London with the Reynolds family. After lunch he was able to tell Sue and Paul about his strange phone call.

'We must pray that this crank makes a mistake and gets caught,' said Sue.

'It was good that you managed to find God's peace as you prayed that evening and didn't lose any sleep,' added Paul.

The Monday and Tuesday saw training preparations reach their goal. Now it was all down to the 800 metres the next day. Just before dinner that evening, however, Tim Horsfell was grim-faced as he drew Gordon aside.

'I'm afraid it's up to you tomorrow, boy. Sam Lewis has gone down with a hamstring injury and the doctor has ruled him out of the final.'

The Dream is Tested

'Conditions are not good this morning,' observed Weston Chadwick, Secretary of the British Olympic Team, at breakfast. 'It's going to be hard on all competitors, track or field.'

A glance at the rain streaks on the dining room window bore out the truth of his words. Glorious Greece was wearing a frown for the first time since the start of the games.

Gordon found encouragement from many letters and cards sent by well-wishers. Amongst them, two were of special significance; a short note from his parents reminding him that everyone in the scattered north coast village was thinking of him, and a card with a bright eyed golden Labrador, like Mega, on it to assure Gordon of the prayers of Sue and Paul and the children.

Conditions had not improved much as the competitors arrived for the 800 metres.

In the dressing room there was quietness as the runners stripped for action. Like the other coaches, Tim Horsfell was talking to his man, reminding him of all the tactics they'd gone over in training. He pointed out particular features of different runners and above all, encouraged Gordon to relax as the tension built up.

Soon it was time to go out and face the large crowd packing the stadium. Banners were everywhere and the cheers going up from every part of the ground reminded runners that they carried the hopes of their respective nations as they ran.

The men lined up, twelve of them in all, and tensed their muscles as they waited for the starter's pistol. CR-AK. The athletes moved swiftly forward, all except one who rushed ahead almost like a sprinter.

Gordon Fraser's concentration had slipped at the split second before the gun was fired and he had gone off at the wrong speed. Like a singer starting on a note too high he felt trapped, the victim of his mistake. The young man's mind was in a frenzy. He kept cramming on the speed and, although he was opening up a remarkable gap between himself and the others, it could only be a matter of time before he ran out of steam and the others caught him.

At the bell, Gordon had a lead of about fifteen metres, but the strain was beginning to tell. He decided to keep the pace up as long as he could. If nothing else he could serve as something of a pacemaker for the others and help them improve their performances.

As for his own, he would just run and run as best he could. About two hundred metres from home, Gordon saw out of the corner of his eye that the Russian, Seznitsm, was coming alongside him, for nearly thirty metres he held him stride for stride, but steadily the Russian pulled away.

There was still second place and the silver medal to fight for, and Gordon gave it everything he had, but about one hundred metres from the tape Fitzgerald, the world champion from the USA, passed him.

His heart thumping and eyes blurred, Gordon pressed on, determined to bring home the bronze medal. If only that finishing tape would not keep moving away. He was no more than ten metres from the tape when Kanato of Kenya passed him to snatch the bronze.

Gordon crashed to the track with his last effort which carried him over the line. As he lay there gasping for breath he felt so disappointed that he had misjudged the start. Yet he had given everything. He could do no more. Tim Horsfell put his arm around the Scot's shoulder and motioned him to save his energy as he tried to gasp an apology.

'I know what went wrong, and it would have been very difficult to undo it. You didn't win a medal but you've one consolation. That cracking pace you set saw to it that Seznitsm won in a new world record time. In those conditions that's remarkable. You didn't win but you certainly achieved something.'

Gordon clung to these words of a wise coach. He had done his best and someone else had benefited. That must be the thing that mattered most.

There were other words that were coming to mean even more to him – the words of the Bible. It was hard to think that when you became the friend of the Lord who created heaven and earth that you could ever have any problems again. But as he read the gospels Gordon saw that Jesus himself had many problems.

The crucifixion seemed to be the end for Jesus. It was only afterwards when he was raised from death that people realised he had been right all along, and that God approved of all he had said and done.

Furthermore, Jesus promised his followers that things wouldn't always seem to go well for them either, but if they kept trusting in him they would see his purpose of good work in their lives. Time and again Jesus urged his disciples to be 'of good cheer', to be confident, for he would always be with them.

On the Thursday and Friday, Gordon kept his mind on the coaching of Tim Horsfell as they worked together on the last details of his preparation. He coped with the occasional loaded question of a sports reporter who had doubts about Gordon's ability to represent the country at this level. The fact was that no other British 1500 metre runner had qualified for the final.

There was something else that proved more difficult to cope with, however. On the Saturday morning amongst the notes from the well-wishers, Gordon found another note from the poison pen. The note said: 'Beware of the son of the ancient ones. Today you will die and we are even.'

Gordon had handled these threats very well, but with all the tension of the final in front of him he began to feel distinctly uneasy. He had to talk with Paul and Sue Reynolds, so he slipped away to their hotel after breakfast.

'It's very puzzling,' commented Paul. 'He must be staying here in London to get the timing of these letters and phone calls just right.'

'Interpol have established that there is no connection between any member of the Dutch team and the Der Antieken gang,' said Gordon, 'and, as you said, Paul, the name "Antieken" is Dutch for "ancient", so there can be no doubt that some friend or friends of the gang are determined to get even with me for my part in their capture.'

Sue Reynolds eyes were full of sympathy. 'You must be feeling terrible with all this going on,' she commented as she poured tea for Gordon.

The runner nodded, but added firmly, 'I never cease to be amazed by how much the Lord has strengthened me through all this. Here I am facing a death threat that can't be ignored, yet my faith in God is growing all the time.'

They prayed together and Gordon returned to the team hotel, where he showed the anonymous note to Tim Horsfell. He insisted that they inform the police, but Gordon was adamant that he would run in the final.

'That crook wants to scare me off and I'm not giving in to that,' he said firmly.

'We'll make that clear to them, son,' agreed Tim, 'and I'm sure they'll agree. The trouble is that I'll need to tell our own committee, and I'm not sure that they will be happy for you to run. After all, they are responsible for your safety.'

'Do we have to tell them yet?' pleaded Gordon weakly.

'Lad, I'm as keen as you are to win the race. I never wanted to see a runner win more than you, after all the hassle you've had, but I'd be breaking my trust and letting everyone down. You wouldn't expect me to do that, would you?'

The young man shook his head. He must wait and see how the police and committee would respond to his plea to be allowed to run. Meanwhile he must concentrate his attention on the race he might lose even before the starter's pistol was fired.

Of all the runners in the race, six had already broken the record set at the previous Olympics four years earlier. They were Mueller of Germany, the fastest 1500 metres runner in Europe, Castelan, a local hero from London and one of the brightest prospects for the future, Yastin of Russia, Ekpen of Kenya, and the two Americans Johnnie Heidekker and Greg Alvis, the favourite to land the gold medal in this brilliant field.

The 1500 metres wasn't even Gordon's favourite race. It might be that when the honours were being handed out he wouldn't be missed anyway. But none of that mattered. What had once been a young man's dream to compete had become a Christian's determination to conquer every problem and win if at all possible. This determination drove out even the very real fear that he might lose his life in a terrible drama which had begun on the quiet moors and bays of his native Highlands, and could explode finally on the television screens of the world.

'Mr Chadwick and the Olympic Committee want to see you now, Gordon.' The tone of Tim Horsfell's voice and the sad look in his eyes told their own story and Gordon was not surprised to hear the decision.

'Gordon,' began Mr Chadwick, 'we take this threat against your life seriously. We cannot allow you to risk your life in the race today.'

'But, Mr Chadwick,' broke in Gordon, 'the Committee must realise that I take this threat seriously too. Do you think this killer is going to give up and go home just because we cheat him today?

'No, he's going to come after me again. I'll never be safe. If you start running away from evil it only chases you faster. Today just before the race, both during and after, the police have a great chance to pick up this man and trace the other gang members he knows.'

The Committee chairman, Col. Wilson, was about to argue when the Chief of Police spoke.

'Mr Fraser is right. This is the best chance we will ever have to trace this evil gang and root them out for good, however dangerous. We will do our best, but if the killer is desperate enough...' The Police Chief's voice trailed away as he looked questioningly at the athlete.

He was a hard-nosed policeman in a country where police were tough and sportsmen were, well sportsmen. He was not used to this sort of determination and death-defying public spirit from a young man who made no money out of running.

'There is no question of our permitting this at all. The lad's safety is our main responsibility. Winning medals or catching crooks is of secondary importance,' stated Col. Wilson.

'I appreciate what you're saying, sir,' replied Gordon, 'but the crook or crank or whatever he is has to be caught. I think there's more chance of that happening here in London today, than at some later stage, somewhere else. Besides, winning medals is also important. I'm very unwilling to hand my chance of winning one over to a gangster.'

The debate flowed backwards and forwards, until eventually Tim Horsfell broke in.

'Ladies and Gentlemen, if we don't make a decision soon we'll be too late. The race starts in one-and-a-half hours and we need to get down to the stadium.'

Some members of the Committee were still very reluctant, but at last they relented and Gordon was allowed to run. Tim Horsfell felt sorry for him.

During the discussion in the Committee he had changed his mind about Gordon running. No athlete should have to compete in circumstances like these. He had secretly hoped for Gordon's own sake that the

Committee would forbid him to run. He admired the young man greatly and liked him, but no one, he felt could run to the best of his ability in these conditions. The coach kept his reservations to himself and did all in his power to get Gordon into the right mental attitude for the race.

The British runner had been the last to appear in the dressing room and last to get out on to the track to limber up. He saw right away that the stadium was even fuller than usual. The 1500 metres was one of the most popular track events and few of those who had come to the Games were going to miss out on it.

High up in one of the grandstands sat the Reynolds. They cheered as soon as they saw Gordon appear on the track, and then joined their chorus to the roar of the crowd as the runners made their way to the starting line.

'Who is number three?' asked Gillian.

'That's Ekpen of Kenya,' replied Dad, 'and number four is Yashtin of Russia.'

'Which number is Gordon?' asked Michelle excitedly.

Mum laughed. 'Why, he's number nine, dear,' she said reaching for the programme.

'It's a good thing we have a programme, Mummy,' said Mike, who was getting so excited he could hardly sit still.

'Yes, agreed Mum. 'It gives a lot of interesting information about each runner and the events they are competing in here in London. Here's one Klaus Mueller, born 10th August 1989, Hamburg, Germany. He isn't competing in any other event, but at the last Olympics he ran in both the 800 and 1500 metres. He didn't win a medal in either, though he reached the final of each.'

'Nevertheless, he did well,' said Paul, 'he was still quite young.'

Then Sue's voice dropped to a whisper. 'Paul, look at this,' she said.

'What is it?' said Paul nonchalantly reaching for the programme.

'Look,' she gasped. 'Look.'

The Killer Makes His Move

Paul Reynolds grabbed the programme and glanced at the name his wife was pointing to with a trembling finger. It was the name of the American runner Greg Alvis. But it was the middle name that almost leapt out from the page as he read it. It was "Der Antieken."

'You stay with the children,' whispered Paul, 'I'll try to get the race stopped.'

'Hurry,' said Sue, 'they're about to start.

Paul quickly approached a policeman on duty and asked to talk with the officials, briefly explaining the problem. The policeman took him down to the track but it was too late, for the starting pistol had fired and the race was under way.

'Quickly, you must stop the race,' insisted Paul to the steward in charge at the track-side. 'One of the athletes is in serious danger; an attempt might be made on his life during the race.'

The steward wondered what Paul was talking about and was on the point of dismissing him as a crank, when the Chief of Police came running up, accompanied by Col. Wilson.

'We saw you talking to the steward,' explained Col. Wilson, who recognised Paul from the media coverage of the bullion robbery. 'We guessed it might be important.'

Paul began to explain why the race should be stopped.

By this time the runners had nearly completed the first lap of the race. Mueller had taken the lead, closely followed by Heidekker and Ekpen. The rest of the runners were in a bunch behind these three and somewhere in the middle was Gordon, quite unaware of the drama unfolding on the track-side.

Tucked in behind Gordon was Greg Alvis, who had positioned himself quite deliberately behind the British runner. There was anger in his narrowed eyes, for though he had never met Gordon, he was well aware of the part he had played in exposing his uncle.

Alvis knew all about the daring bullion robbery, for he had been involved in it himself. In fact, his speed had been important in helping to make the operation so successful, and he had been looking for a large slice of the stolen money for himself. Now, thanks to this man who was pounding round the track ahead of him, he would get nothing. Not only that, but Gordon Fraser himself might get a reward for helping to catch the gang. The American was determined that Gordon should receive no such reward.

But what was happening at the track-side? The steward in charge of the race was arguing with the Chief of Police. Could the authorities possibly suspect what was going to happen? How could they? He had told no-one. He had threatened his victim, but how could he possibly suspect him.

Alvis had intended to wait until the third lap of the race before dealing with Gordon, but now that he sensed the race might be stopped, he decided to make a move as soon as possible. Using his left thumb he pressed the underside of the ring he was wearing. Slowly, the top of the ring opened to reveal a short, sharp point.

Alvis lengthened his stride and made to overtake the British runner. His plan was to 'accidentally' stab Gordon as he passed. The American had forgotten one thing, however. As the favourite to win the race, he had the eyes of most of the other runners on him, and when he made his move, the others behind began to move too.

As Alvis pulled out to pass Gordon, Castelan, the Greek runner, went with him, accidentally catching the American's left arm. Alvis was punched by his own clenched fist which he was ready to hit Gordon with. Immediately he felt the pain and realised what had happened. In blind panic he swung his ringed hand at the British athlete, missed him and overbalanced, bringing down both Gordon and Castelan with his fallen body.

The stunned roar of the crowd was punctuated by the sharp scream of Greg as he lay writhing on the track while police and officials gathered around him. Castelan, too, was out of the race having spiked himself with his own running shoe when he fell.

Gordon Fraser had struggled to his feet, trying to shake off the effects of shock and pain, and was chasing the rest of the runners who were by now nearly half a lap clear.

'Looks·like I've had it,' he muttered through gritted teeth. Yet he didn't feel discouraged. There was still plenty time to do his best and that was all God asked.

Thinking of God prompted the young Christian to pray for courage, confidence and the will to win. How many obstacles he had to overcome to even get to the final. Now he had suffered a fall that would have finished most other runners. Perhaps there would be no more hindrances as he mounted one last determined attempt to bring home a gold medal.

Gordon could barely hear the cries of the American athlete behind him as he threw tactics to the wind and sprinted forward. He had no idea of the drama that was unfolding as the American was carried off the track surrounded by supporters.

'I am poisoned,' whined Alvis. 'My ring. It was full of deadly poison.'

'What are you talking about?' stammered the United States trainer.

'Hurry!' whispered the stricken athlete in fear. 'My life's in danger from that poison. It acts real fast.'

'What's all this?' rasped Col. Wilson, his suspicions aroused.

'I tried to get Fraser with the poison but I hit myself in the crush. I need an antidote fast or I'll die.'

Race officials stood around in confusion. Reporters and photographers responded more quickly than the others, noting the dramatic details of the bullion robbery plan as they spilled from the mouth of the panic-stricken runner. Names and rackets of the whole Der Antieken gang were disclosed as police questioned the stricken man.

There were people in high places, even eminent names within international law enforcement. The Police Chief was staggered by what he heard but moved quickly as possible to relay the information to relevant agencies and forces.

By the time he was whisked off to hospital to receive the life-giving antidote, Greg Alvis had uncovered the whole network of crime, which was going on both in Europe and in the United States of America. As a reporter put it later, 'This one athlete stumbled and brought a whole race of crooks down with him.'

Meanwhile, back on track the 1500 metres was into its third lap, for most runners at least. Gordon was slowly making up lost ground but was nearly a hundred metres behind the leaders, who were least aware of the event nearby. Mueller was still in the lead, Ekpen of Kenya was in second place and Yashtin of Russia, third. Heidekker was tiring and most of the others were slowly, but definitely losing touch with the frontrunners.

Gordon pounded on relentlessly, first closing the gap on the stragglers then, painfully slowly, edging his way past one after another throughout the third lap until at the bell he was catching Heidekker who was twenty metres adrift of the leaders. The race had been run at a good pace, with Mueller's efforts ensuring that a world record time was within reach of a determined finisher. The German himself was now tiring rapidly and Ekpen went to the front followed by Yashtin.

His eyes beginning to blur with the effort he was putting in, Gordon Fraser prayed for strength for one last lap of all-out effort. With his arms flailing vigorously he passed the fading Mueller on the back straight and battled on in pursuit of the two men who were contesting the lead at the front.

Both Ekpen and Yashtin were great runners at this distance and each dearly wanted to win for his country. With the Americans nowhere and Mueller spent, the two men sensed the race was wide open for either of them to win. Coming out of the last bend with 200 metres to run they were both ten metres clear of the determined figure in third place who had the British contingent on their feet as he ran on, almost by instinct.

To finish as best he could was uppermost in Gordon's mind as he pressed legs and lungs through the last fiery discipline of an unforgettable running season. Yashtin was tiring. Settling for the silver medal he fell back, releasing himself from the tension of total effort. Twenty metres from home the Kenyan champion sensed he had broken Yashtin's challenge and allowed his aching body a fraction's respite as he strode for the tape.

Ekpen raised his arms in a victory salute and that very action prevented him from seeing the figure of Gordon coming up to cross the line with him.

It had been a long, hard race, yet it required a photograph to decide who had won. Not that Gordon Fraser was showing a great deal of concern about gold medals. He lay on the track exhausted and panting for breath. Tim Horsfell rushed over to the group of athletes gathering around him.

'Stand back, stand back,' he shouted. 'Give him air.' Turning to his athlete he said, 'Unbelievable! That was unbelievable, Gordon. You came from nowhere.'

Tim Horsfell's words were drowned in a massive cheer from the crowd as the electronic scoreboard declared the final result. The photo finish placed Gordon Fraser first. As he fell over the line he must have breasted the electronic tape fractionally ahead of the Kenyan.

It was a wonderful victory, for so much had been against it ever coming to pass; the lack of training facilities, the harrowing spell in captivity, the death threats, the unwillingness of the officials to let him run and finally the fall that sent him crashing to the ground. Gordon Fraser had overcome all these things to win, and he had done it with God's help.

As he lay there on the track slowly getting his breath back Gordon thought of gold. There were the bars he had found in the broch as they uncovered the crime of the dangerous gang. There was the medal that would soon be in his hand, hard won and precious.

But it was a different gold that stood out most in his thoughts at that moment, the gold of a living relationship with God that would go far beyond the Olympic race track, taking him through the whole of his life and leading him he knew not where. That too was gold, true gold. He felt he understood so clearly a song that he had recently heard: 'I'd rather have Jesus than silver or gold.'

In the few hours that followed, leading up to and including the medal presentation, Gordon came to realise how much his life was touching that of other people. Tim Horsfell and the other British athletes, the Olympic Committee members, the British press, all shared in his success and enjoyed it as if it were their own. As he stood to attention for the National Anthem, Gordon realised that, in a sense, a whole nation shared his triumph, and at that moment as never before his life belonged to other people.

When Jesus Christ came into the world he came not for himself but for others. His whole life was taken up by meeting their needs and making a way of salvation for them. He lived, died and rose again for others. That was why God sent him. Yet Jesus lived a life full of joy, even with all the suffering he had; and he had said to his followers, 'As the Father sent me, so I send you.'

Gordon could look forward to joy in his Christian life, but it would be the joy of service, not the pleasure of selfishness.

The strains of the National Anthem drew to a close and the crowd cheered. Gordon shook hands with Ekpen and Yashtin, the other medal winners who shared the podium with him. On the way back to the pavilion Tim Horsfell brought the young athlete up to date with all that had happened off the track during the dramatic race.

'So Greg Alvis was the man,' said Gordon in amazement. 'I can hardly believe it.'

Horsfell went on, 'the remarkable thing is that Alvis, who was Der Antieken's nephew, was heavily into organised crime and has given the police valuable information they might never have got hold of any other way. The police are busy right now rounding up a whole range of individuals they had long suspected of involvement, but whom they could never pin anything on.'

Then, looking at Gordon in a funny sort of way, he added, 'Imagine you stumbling on all this when you were training on a Highland beach.'

'That's where it all happens,' laughed Gordon. 'We can't all live sheltered lives like you London boys.

The Reward

The minibus wound its way westward along the coast from Thurso, its occupants becoming more excited with every mile that passed. Just outside the village the driver turned off the main road and drove the short distance to the cottage by the moor. He parked the minibus and allowed the passengers to alight.

'That's where it all started, Paul,' said Sue. 'Who would have thought when we came here a month ago that we would get involved in tracking down a criminal gang.'

'And meeting an athlete who would save a girl's life, get us free seats at the Olympics and win a gold medal. Don't forget that,' replied Paul with a laugh.

'Hold on there,' said Gordon. 'I didn't do these things. Well, not alone. God was helping and it was you folks who taught me to trust God.'

'You played your part too, Mega,' said Jason, fondling the Labrador's big ears. The dog barked and wagged her tail. She was delighted to be back in this land of adventure and rabbits, especially rabbits.

'We must go, Gordon,' said Mr Fraser Senior, nodding towards the village. 'The people will be waiting.'

Taking Gordon's mother by the arm, his dad led the way back to the minibus. Soon all were aboard and heading back to the main road. Before long they were descending the hill into the village.

Bettyhill was strangely quiet until they arrived at the centre, which was built around the Post Office and shop, the village hall and school. All these things had their place in the memories of the local boy who had brought such credit to his home. There was a bunting of red, white and blue hung across the street, and they could hear the local pipe band beginning to play as the bus turned the corner towards the village hall.

The Highlanders are not an excitable people, but the faces of the crowd displayed the happy pride of men and women who knew that, in a real sense, Gordon Fraser had done it for them as well as for Britain – and for God.

There was a huge cheer as Gordon stepped down from the bus, and eager hands grasped those of the Reynolds, who had become very popular in the village. The driver had parked his minibus only about ten yards from the hall door, yet such was the crush of villagers and others wanting to congratulate their hero and his parents, that it took more than half an hour for them all to reach the refuge of the hall.

Inside, the room was decorated with balloons and paper streamers depicting the five inter-twining circles of the Olympic symbol. There was a large picture of Gordon receiving his gold medal and a 'Welcome Home' slogan above it. Tables were set neatly and carefully, covering every spare metre of floor space. Nearly three hundred people were seated by the time Gordon and the others were led to the top table by Rob Mackay, the piping instructor, playing a suitable air on his pipes.

A brief welcome was given by Charlie Macrae, a local man who was good with words and who told a few funny stories that had the whole company laughing happily.

Macrae then introduced the local minister, a popular Irishman named Matthew Best, who led them in prayer and thanked God for all that he had done amongst them in recent days. He concluded by asking a blessing on the food they were going to eat and the meal got under way.

The Reynolds children and Michelle found it an unforgettable day, for the hospitality of the north is even more special for children than adults. There was an abundance of good things to eat and each child received a gift to play with or use, that would keep the memory of Bettyhill fresh with them for a very long time.

When the meal was over Charlie Macrae called for attention and began to speak.

'As we all know,' he said, 'these have been momentous days for our small community. We've all known Gordon since he was a boy and, in a sense, it's no surprise to us that he won an Olympic medal. We always knew he was good.

'Mind you, when we saw the television coverage of the training methods of those chaps in Africa and America, we realised it would be hard for Gordon. All he has had to train on is the local beach. Still, as my grandmother used to say, "There's something special about that sand. At least it's better than the sand along the coast at Tongue."'

This statement was greeted by laughter from the whole company, including one man whose chortle strongly resembled the braying of a donkey. Mike and Michelle found this so funny that they only managed to stop laughing with the greatest of difficulty. Charlie Macrae continued.

'We knew Gordon was a great athlete and it's a good thing for the village to see him bring home a gold medal.'

Loud cheers filled the hall and Gordon responded to calls from all over the hall by bringing out his medal and holding it up for all to see.

'What we didn't know until Sergeant Wallace told us,' added Macrae, 'was that this first class athlete was also a budding detective. Along with our good friends, the Reynolds, Gordon helped to capture a dangerous gang of gold thieves.'

There were more cheers and applause which only died down when the chairman raised his hand.

'The whole country knows about these things,' he went on, 'but what very few people know is that Gordon and the Reynolds family have received a reward for their heroism. What's more, they are giving it to this village.'

There were sighs of amazement from the packed audience. Charlie Macrae motioned to Gordon to explain.

'It's very simple really. When Paul Reynolds and I were told about the reward, Paul suggested that it really belongs to Bettyhill, because these crooks disgraced the village with their evil exploits. What we want to see done with the reward money is the building of an all-purpose sports centre for the young people of the north. There would be a good running track amongst other things, so that budding athletes would have the same chance of being selected as those in the cities.'

The idea met with the obvious approval of the local people, especially the younger ones. At this point Paul Reynolds stood up and spoke.

'We realised that if this arrangement was going to work we would need to find a suitable person to be in charge of the sports centre. We've thought about it and it seems to me there's only one person for this job. I have to admit I haven't consulted him about this idea, but I can't think of anyone better suited for this work than Gordon himself.'

The look of surprise on the athlete's face proved that the idea had never crossed his mind. Paul's suggestion, however, had plenty of support amongst the villagers, for they saw that no one could be better for the task than an Olympic gold medallist who knew the area so well.

'One other thing we hope to do,' added Paul Reynolds, 'is to get one or two chalets built in the village so that holidays can be provided for families. This is a lovely place, and with a sports centre it would be a great attraction for young families. I know that we as a family will remember this holiday. There's something special about this whole place and it would be great for more young families to be able to enjoy it.'

People were impressed that two young men were prepared to give away such a large reward to help the village and others who would come to it. They were doing what they could to see that the name of Bettyhill, which had been on everyone's lips during the bullion adventure, should continue to be special to some who might otherwise never see it. And it would be great if another Olympic athlete could be found on that rugged northern coast.

The reception over, the people made their way slowly outside, where most stood around in groups talking happily about all that had taken place that evening.

'Where's Jason, Mum?' asked Gillian.

'I don't know. I saw him a few minutes ago with Mega. Aren't they here?' Gillian looked around, but Jason and Mega were nowhere to be seen. Then a thought struck her.

'That's where they'll be,' she said.

'Where?' asked her mum. 'Gillian, Gillian!'

But Gillian was off at speed in the direction of the beach. Sure enough, she saw in the distance a boy and his dog running across the deserted sand. There they were, the two who had started it all, the vigilant Labrador and her adventurous brother. Where would the Amsterdam bullion be at that very moment if they hadn't been faithful and firm to the end?

Once they had been alone. No one had believed them. Not even their parents, not even Gillian herself she recalled with shame. Faith in God had kept Jason going, and God had guided the young lad, answering his prayers.

God had answered Gillian's prayers too and as she ran across the beach after her brother, she knew that God would always be with her as she grew up. She might never be rich, but she would always have the true gold of a loving relationship with her Heavenly Father.

If you have enjoyed this book
then look out for the other titles in
this series by Cliff Rennie:

ISBN 978-1-87167-647-1

ISBN 978-1-87167-669-3

CHRISTIAN FOCUS PUBLICATIONS

Christian Focus · Christian Heritage · CF4K · Mentor

Christian Focus Publications publishes books for adults and children under its four main imprints: Christian Focus, Christian Heritage, CF4K and Mentor. Our books reflect that God's word is reliable and Jesus is the way to know him, and live for ever with him.

Our children's publication list includes a Sunday school curriculum that covers pre-school to early teens; puzzle and activity books. We also publish personal and family devotional titles, biographies and inspirational stories that children will love.

If you are looking for quality Bible teaching for children then we have an excellent range of Bible story and age specific theological books.

From pre-school to teenage fiction, we have it covered!

Find us at our web page: www.christianfocus.com

CF4·K
Because you're never
too young to know Jesus